Sarah's Reluctant Duke

THE HEIR AND THE SPARE
BOOK ONE

FIONA MIERS

Chapter One

London 1812

Lord Oliver Lyre, the newly-inherited tenth Duke of Lincoln, let his eyes be drawn to a corner of the ballroom where the birthday girl stood. If the ball hadn't been in honour of Lady Charlotte Dunford—the little sister he'd never had—he would not have attended. Lady Charlotte was the younger sister of his best friend, Sir John Dunford, son of the Duke of Arrow.

Oliver smiled as he watched her moving about the room, a sense of pride and love warming his chest. She'd grown into a lovely young woman. He'd known Charlotte since she was in short skirts, running around the grounds showing off her ankles. She had always treated him like she had treated her brother—with unwaning, absolute hatred one day and intense affection the next. Oliver had only his elder brother Gerald for company, who had seen the younger Oliver as well beneath him.

Unfortunately, due to a tragic carriage accident, his absent father and his indifferent brother had passed together, leaving Oliver with a title he neither coveted nor felt worthy of.

He hated it, in fact. The attention of the ton, mothers trying to marry off their daughters to him, the huge amount of work involved in owning multiple estates, looking after so many tenants... It had only been a year since he'd inherited the title and he'd already sworn off most ton events.

Lady Charlotte, the little brat, had used every trick she possessed, including fake tears, pleading, and even threats, to get Oliver to attend her twenty-first birthday. He, of course, had succumbed. It would take a force of nature to stop Charlotte when she had her mind set on something.

"Excuse me." Oliver turned and bowed to the two gentlemen with whom he had been speaking moments earlier, before making his way across the room to where Charlotte stood, holding court.

The crowd parted in front of him like the Red Sea before Moses. Oliver's heart sank, and he couldn't stop the sigh that escaped. He missed being the second son, relatively unimportant and unnoticed by the haut ton. He'd have given absolutely anything to have Gerald back, even with his brother's indifference to Oliver's existence. Gerald had known how to behave; how to be the esteemed holder of a dukedom. He'd been raised for it——bred for it, even. How he would have laughed to see Oliver struggle with the responsibility.

A wry smile crept onto Oliver's face as he thought about his deceased elder brother, and he drew up next to the now-unoccupied Charlotte.

"My lady." Oliver leaned closer than was proper and spoke directly into her ear.

"My lord!" Charlotte spun to face him and greeted him with a smile that was both warm and genuine.

The icy discomfort he'd been feeling from the moment he entered the room melted away. Lady Charlotte was worth the pain. She would never be one to call him by his brother's title, and he would be forever grateful for that.

"May I claim my dance? I do believe this is ours." Oliver extended his arm and grinned at the woman he saw as his surrogate sister. An action he knew would cause the dimple in his right cheek to become pronounced.

"Of course." Charlotte took his arm.

Swinging her into the perfect waltz position that included at least six inches between their bodies and no hands below the waist, he looked down at her laughing blue eyes and mock-scowled at her.

"Having fun, are you?" He didn't even attempt a polite start to the conversation now that they were out of general earshot.

She giggled, and once again Oliver struggled with the frustration he felt at his position.

"Of course, I am. It's my birthday. How are you enjoying my night, Oliver? There are so many eligible young ladies in this room that I expected you to have run away screaming by now." Charlotte spoke with her characteristic bluntness.

"You mean to torture me, then?"

Charlotte smiled slowly, appearing to think deeply about her answer.

"I have been hoping you may find a wife, yes. You need to spend more time consorting with ladies rather than the type of women I hear you and my brother have been consorting with lately."

"That is none of your business, scamp," Oliver hissed at Charlotte through his teeth. What sort of lady would say that to a gentleman?

"Which part? The part where I said you should marry?" She emphasized the word with a cheeky smile. "Or the part where I mentioned the not-so-ladylike women you frequently visit?"

Oliver gasped and only just stopped himself from taking a step back. Girls of Charlotte's social rank were not meant to know about such women, let alone speak about them. Was this the same girl who had put worms under his pillow and cried on his lap when she'd scraped her knees running down a path? Impossible.

"Lady Charlotte! You shouldn't speak of it. I'm barely six and twenty, hardly old enough for you to be marrying me off to some title-adoring, bird-brained, barely-out-of-the-school-room debutante."

Oliver took a deep breath as he struggled to hold in his frustration. He knew he had to marry a woman who would be an appropriate duchess, but he wasn't ready, or willing. Not yet. After already being forced into a role he didn't want, husband was a role he could do without for a few more years.

Charlotte laughed with delight, obviously pleased at getting the reaction she'd anticipated.

Time for a change of subject, I think.

"What about you, scamp? Are you planning on finding a husband this season? You are getting a little long in the tooth compared to some of these pretty young faces I see tonight." He liked turning the tables on the quick-witted Lady Charlotte Dunford, even though his jibes were empty and they both knew it. With Charlotte's handsome face, pleasing figure, sharp wit and generous dowry, she'd still be good marriage material when she was one and thirty.

"Do not even think of turning it back on me, Lord Oliver," she said, addressing him by his former title and therefore pleasing him greatly. "We both know that I'll marry as soon as I find someone who is remotely interesting." Charlotte managed to laugh softly and shrugged one creamy shoulder.

Oliver cocked his head and tried to see Charlotte as a marriageable woman, rather than the younger sister he'd always wanted. She was beautiful in a dark-haired, pale-skinned, classic sort of way. Her curvaceous figure wasn't precisely in fashion but was certainly pleasing. Her rather ample breasts swelled up from her low neckline.

If Oliver hadn't known her for most of his life, then he would likely have found her desirable. She was intelligent, and not in any way flighty. A plus on both accounts. He couldn't stand a woman whose main goal in life was to be a lovely ornament on a shelf.

"It's a pity I can't marry you, Charlotte. You would make me the perfect duchess."

Charlotte laughed without humour and Oliver could understand why. Unlike him, she'd never had a reprieve from the bevy of suitors at her doorstep. She had been courted since her coming out by men who wanted her for breeding, as well as her dowry.

"I know, Lord Oliver, if only I could stand the idea of marrying you."

Oliver laughed wholeheartedly, ignoring the glances that swung their way. He did love this girl.

They finished their waltz and he walked her over to the edge of the ballroom with almost every eye in the room following them. Oliver tried his best to ignore the attention.

He turned his head and spotted a rather large matron towing not one, but two daughters in her wake. It was time to remove himself from the reach of this possible matchmaker. He had no intention of being anyone's target this evening.

"Kindly allow me to take my leave, Lady Charlotte. Would you forgive me for taking a walk around the gardens?" Oliver started bowing before he had even finished his sentence.

Charlotte glanced over his shoulder at the woman making a direct line through the crowd for them and chuckled.

"Go, go," she urged discreetly. "Just don't get caught compromising anyone."

Oliver didn't even break stride as he simultaneously scowled over his shoulder at Charlotte and made his escape from the room. He could still hear her tinkling laughter as he exited into the gardens.

~

"ARE these not the most beautiful gardens you have ever seen, Mr. Millington?" Sarah Collins turned to her handsome escort for the night, enchanted by her unfamiliar surroundings.

It had been such a lovely suggestion of Mr. Millington's for her to get some fresh air. London truly was a wonder and she had not expected such a delightful garden space in the middle of such a large city.

"No one in Somerset has gardens such as these. Imagine the time and care it must have taken the gardeners."

Mr. Patrick Millington had spent the previous two weeks courting Sarah and she rather liked him. He was untitled but wealthy enough for her family's needs due to an inheritance he had recently acquired. Millington came from a good family—and if the gossip was to be believed— was well-educated and loved horses. As did Sarah.

Although he did talk about himself and his horses a little too often for her liking, Sarah didn't perceive that to be an insurmountable problem. After all, how often would she be conversing with her husband once they were married? Surely not much, except for over the dinner table? She could handle that.

"They are handsome gardens indeed, Miss Collins," he agreed, glancing over his shoulder toward the ballroom. Sarah noticed where Millington's gaze landed and she stopped short, her stomach jumping. They were much further away from the safety of the crowded ballroom than she had at first realized. Her mother would be wondering where she was.

"Oh." Sarah turned, one hand landing on her throat as she smiled up at the large man next to her. "I didn't realize we were so far from the house, Mr. Millington. Shall we return?" She could smell the sweet stench of liquor on his breath as he bent his head in her direction. She would have gagged if she had not taken a quick step sideways.

"In a moment." Mr. Millington's cold hands came up to grip the tops of her bare arms and Sarah winced as his touch gripped tight and turned painful.

He twisted her arms, forcing her back up against a tree. The bark scratched against her bare skin.

"Ow." She blinked back sudden hot tears. "You're hurting me. Let go this instant, Mr. Millington!"

Instead of complying, he crashed his mouth down onto hers.

Sarah's heart, instead of jumping for joy at a sign of affection, leapt in fear. She struggled, squirming her head from side to side and trying to wriggle out of his hold. But he had such a firm grip on her, she couldn't break free. Horror sprung up. When he forced his slimy tongue into her mouth, she could taste the acidic alcohol and gagged.

Enough!

As her supposed suitor moved one hand to her breast and squeezed roughly, causing pain to shoot through her tender flesh, Sarah bit down on the offensive tongue invading her mouth.

When Millington drew back in shock she managed to turn her head away. Her chest heaved as she drew air into her starving lungs.

"Stop," she cried, pushing at his heavy form. "You must let me go."

Why was he doing this? Things had been going well up until this point. What had changed?

"I think I deserve a taste of this body before I decide if we are getting leg-shackled, don't you?" He spoke gruffly, his hot breath putrid against her turned cheek and ear.

Undeterred by her obvious distress, he began pulling down her bodice with one hand and feeling under her skirt with his other. Cold air froze her nipples and panic forced her heart into a gallop.

"No!" Sarah began struggling again, bashing against his solid chest with her clenched fists and simultaneously trying to drag her dress back up to cover her exposed breasts.

Her head flew back against the tree as Millington shoved her. The force was enough for black spots to form at the edges of her vision.

Oh Lord! She couldn't faint. Not now. He might have his way with her and if she wasn't conscious, she couldn't fight back.

Pain splintered across the back of her head as she fought to stay awake. Fabric ripped and cool air brushed her ribs.

I refuse to let this happen, she thought, desperate to stop him any way she could.

She let herself go limp against him, closing her eyes against the dulling pain in her head and quietly gathering her remaining strength. When he moved away to fumble with his trousers, she raised her hands and leapt forward. She forced her pointed fingers into his eye sockets, scratching at his eyes with as much force as she could manage. She could feel wet skin and blood beneath her nails, but she didn't stop.

Millington stumbled backwards, letting out a yell, and Sarah picked up her skirts, heedless of the state of her bodice, and ran as fast as she could. Thanking the years she had spent chasing her brothers up and down cobblestone steps, she made a mad dash for her life.

She found a small, dark alcove created by a cluster of dense trees and crouched beneath it, her heaving chest aching in her attempts not to breathe too loudly.

"You little... bitch," came Millington's voice from the darkness.

He walked past the spot where she was hiding, and she held her breath so as not to be heard. Her lungs burned and she bit her bruised lip, tears stinging her eyes.

Her heart hammered in her ears and her body trembled. What would she do if he found her? Could she fight him off again? Cold air shocked her bare skin, but she didn't dare move. Not yet.

After the longest minutes of her life, Millington let out a crude word and stalked back toward the house, mumbling to himself. His footsteps became less audible until finally, Sarah couldn't hear any movement around her at all.

It was only then, when she was sure he was gone, that she let the tears fall, hot and wet against her cheeks. She pulled the remains of her dress together, feelings of disgust and betrayal foremost in her mind. How could a gentleman do such a thing?

Clearly, he was no gentleman after all.

Then came the terrifying realization of what would happen if she were seen now. She would be ruined forever. The weight of her family's future still rested on her shoulders, and within weeks of their arrival in London, she had destroyed everything with her naive trust in the wrong man.

Sarah wrapped her arms around her knees and bent her head, muffling her cries with her skirts, fearful of being heard and unsure how she would ever be able to get herself home.

ONCE HIS IRRITATION HAD RECEDED, Oliver quite enjoyed wandering slowly through the gardens, delaying the inevitable return to the ballroom. Something Charlotte had said had touched a raw nerve inside him.

Back when he was just the second son and not the heir, he had happily conversed with gently-bred females, knowing their mamas would soon steer their attention to someone older or of a higher rank.

He'd pursued a lot of physical ventures also that he no longer had time for. His shoulders, that his tailor had once called too large to be fashionable, were shrinking in size at the lack of activity.

His days as an amateur pugilist and horse rider were behind him, and he wanted nothing more than to have those pastimes back.

He'd missed the chance to find a woman who didn't want him for his rank. Too late to playfully flirt and get to know someone properly. He knew why those women yearned for him now and thanks to a painful twist of fate, he would never know who wanted him for more than his title. Like a prize goose at Christmastime, he could not get away from the hunt fast enough.

Oliver stopped, noticing a strange noise coming from the pathway up ahead of him. Something, or someone, was hiding under or behind a cluster of trees.

"Hello, who's there?" he called out.

There was a loud gasp and then nothing. Lamps were hanging throughout the garden and from where he stood, he could make out a figure in the shadows. He assumed it was a woman hiding there, judging by the little piece of material peeking out from the bush. She seemed to be holding her breath, for now there was no noise coming from behind the trees.

Oliver laughed softly to himself. Maybe an assignation had been organised for this spot? It was certainly far enough away from the house for her and her partner not to be seen.

"Come out, whoever you are," Oliver called again, feeling slightly mischievous.

He would bet that some bored married lady had seen him and jumped behind the bush to preserve her reputation. Maybe he should speak to her. It was probably time he joined the ranks of the 'titled men with a mistress'. He grinned slightly at the cynical thought. What was a duke without a mistress?

A woman crawled out from beneath the trees and slowly stood, holding together the remains of her torn bodice.

"Please, don't hurt me," she whispered, her face hidden, eyes on the ground.

Chapter Two

Struck speechless, his heart lodged in his throat. It seemed no merry wife was hiding in the brush, but a fallen angel. Golden ringlets pulled askew and what was once a pale, virginal ball gown was now dirty and ripped. Too much of her creamy skin had been bared to his gaze for decency, but what caught his eye was the way her cheeks glistened from recently shed tears from her beautiful pale eyes. The young woman had clearly been crying.

He removed his coat immediately to help her cover herself.

Her head lifted a touch and her mouth fell open. As he stepped forward, she took a step back.

"Please, no." She looked positively stricken and began pulling her ruined gown closer around her small body. He couldn't help but notice she had rather full breasts though he tried hard not to look.

Oliver stopped moving and instead just held his jacket out to her like one would to a wounded animal.

It was evident the poor girl had been brutalised. The sick churning in his stomach that had begun at the initial sight of her, intensified as anger set in.

Who would dare touch a creature this beautiful and angelic? She would be lucky to be half the weight of an average man. What chance would she have of defending herself?

"Please, take my jacket." Oliver's voice cracked like a green boy, and he didn't care. "You must be freezing."

New tears welled up in the angel's violet eyes as she reached for his jacket with trembling fingers. Taking it from him, she turned her back to shield herself as she slipped her arms into it.

Oliver gaped at the unsightly red scratches marring the perfect skin of her upper back. Either she had been pushed against a tree or the ground, and in quite a violent manner. Bloody bastard!

"What happened to you?"

The woman turned around. Tears began to slide down her cheeks. Her face crumpled as she sank to her knees.

Oliver rushed forward and dropped to his knees, reaching out and wrapping his arms around her small frame and holding her against his body. She gripped his lapels like a child and cried.

Oliver stroked his angel's soft hair and made soft crooning noises into her ear. She continued to sob against his evening suit. He rarely felt needed by anyone, and it gave him a satisfaction to be able to help someone in such a small, but significant way. Though he would give anything for her not to have endured the violence against her in the first place.

"It's all right, you're safe," he reassured her. Although he had no idea if it was all right, or if it ever could be again. If she'd been molested, he could not imagine a worse fate for a gently-bred woman.

Wiping at her eyes, the woman finally straightened and clamoured to her feet before stepping back from him. He stood too. Despite her red nose and puffy cheeks, he'd never seen anyone more beautiful.

His heart clenched tighter the longer he stared at her. As he handed her his white handkerchief, she rewarded him with a smile. The angel dabbed at her face and wiped her nose before taking a few deep breaths to steady herself.

"Thank you so much, sir. I need to leave before anyone sees me. Can you help me, please?"

"Of course, I can."

Oliver's mind raced with the logistics of how to get her out of the grounds unseen. Why hadn't he thought about that before she mentioned it? He should have been the one to offer practical aid.

"I can't be seen like this." Her voice broke on the words and two fresh, shimmering tears slipped down her cheeks. "No one would ever marry me."

Oliver's heart all but broke at the pitiful look on her face, for it was indeed true. Her beauty and virginity were the two things that would be her greatest assets on the marriage market. If society regarded her as damaged goods, no one of any consequence would marry her, no matter how beautiful she was.

He wasn't having that. Although he'd known the girl only a few minutes, something about her smile, her gentle voice, told him that she was indeed a prize. Sweet, honest, and a rare find. A diamond of the finest quality.

"I'll get you out of here. Let's walk toward the front of the house and you can stay back in the shadows while I arrange a carriage." Oliver offered his arm to the angel, and she took it. He ushered her toward the house.

"I'm Sarah, by the way." She sniffed as she wiped her face again with his now-soaked handkerchief.

"Oh, well..." Oliver stammered, his brain temporarily locking out the ability to speak. How did this rare beauty keep flabbergasting him? He'd never been so verbally incompetent in his life.

"I think we're past polite names, do you not? After all, you have probably seen more of me tonight than anyone should before marriage."

Oliver's mouth dropped open, the trees closing in around him. What had he done?

Her honest, and far too accurate, assessment of the situation was unsettling. If someone saw them in her current state of 'dress', it would be his head on the chopping block, or in the parson's trap as the case may be.

"I'm not interested in getting married," he blurted out. He spoke louder than he should have, grabbing her arm and planting his feet, stopping her in their race to the front entrance.

Sarah chuckled and turned to look up at him, her violet eyes sparkling with the reflected lights from the nearby ballroom.

My God, she's beautiful.

"I didn't mean I wanted to marry you, sir. Just that considering the state you found me in, and after all you have done for me tonight, the least I could do was introduce myself as Sarah and not Miss such and such, daughter of such and such." She sighed loudly and waved her hand in a dismissive way. "I hate all that."

Oliver smiled despite himself. Incredible. Was there a marriageable female in London who didn't care about connections? He frowned as his cynical voice crowded his thoughts. He didn't think she'd feel the same way when they were properly introduced, and that was such a shame. Why couldn't he just be who he'd always been?

"I'm Oliver." He smiled at her, a strange swirling feeling blossoming deep inside him.

He'd never been introduced as just "Oliver" in his entire six and twenty years of life. Even as the spare son he was a lord. What an odd, exhilarating feeling it was. "Oliver" could be anyone, do anything.

"Oliver." She repeated his name. The tone of her voice had a huskiness that sent a bolt of desire to his groin.

"Please wait here, Sarah." He forced himself to let go of her arm and stepped away, needing to put some distance between them.

The last thing he wanted to feel for an almost-ravished woman was desire. The thought disgusted him. She needed his compassion. She need sympathy, not more lust.

Oliver left her near a garden gate and went in search of his cloak and servants, arranging for his carriage to take Sarah home and then come back to retrieve him.

It wasn't the first time Oliver was grateful to have so many people at his disposal, but tonight he'd used his power to help someone other than himself.

Her situation made him want to protect her, go out of his way to help her, and he liked this new side of himself. Somehow, helping Sarah in this way gave him a deep satisfaction, as if his life suddenly had a meaningful purpose.

He stepped back into the crowded, loud ballroom and found his hostess as quickly as possible. He pulled Charlotte aside again, ignoring the look of annoyance the lady she was speaking to shot in his direction.

"Where have you been? And where is your jacket? There has been such a commotion." Charlotte beamed at him, her blue eyes sparkling in the candlelight.

Lady Charlotte knew as any good hostess does, that gossip——either good or bad——was the only real thing that made any ball memorable.

"Patrick Millington came back to the ballroom half an hour ago with blood dripping down his face. He said he was escorting Miss Collins and made a remark to which she took exception and attacked him. I applaud her, really. The man is disgusting, but she shouldn't have gone quite that far." Charlotte started to laugh but stopped short. "What's the matter, Oliver?"

Oliver ground his teeth together, the crunch inside his skull doing nothing to halt the rage from building. He forced the words out. "I found Sarah in the back garden." His hands were clenched into fists at his sides as he realised the attempted seduction of an innocent was going to go completely unreported.

Lady Charlotte gasped and took a small step back, her eyes opening wide as she took in his rage.

"He didn't just say something that offended her. Her bodice was torn apart and her back was scratched." Oliver's chest rapidly rose and fell as he struggled to control his breathing. "Where is that bastard? I'll show him what happens to a man who attacks someone half his size." Turning on his heel, he took a step in the direction of the card room. Millington would pay for this.

"You can't." Lady Charlotte grabbed at his forearm and pulled him back to face her, her grip tight and unforgiving.

"He's already gone home, and you know it would ruin Miss Collins if people found out he stole even a kiss, let alone... more."

Oliver forced himself to think clearly through the red haze engulfing his common sense. Breathing was hard, but he inhaled and exhaled slowly, until relative calm descended. Charlotte was right. She always was. If he made a scene, then his angel would be ruined, and he could not save her from that.

He observed somewhere in his brain that he kept calling her 'his angel'. The pet name seemed too intimate for so short an acquaintance, but with her ethereal glow, golden hair and violet eyes, angelic was the perfect description for her. She was, by far, the most beautiful woman he had ever laid eyes on.

"Fine. You need to tell her mother that she had a sudden headache attack from the cold night air, and she needs to be taken home immediately. I've had my carriage drive around to the side entrance to pick her up, and her mother needs to go to her. Have her wait at the front entrance. I will instruct the carriage to pick up Sarah's mother on the way through to the exit. You need to help her, Charlotte."

"I'll do everything I can, Oliver," she reassured him, giving his forearm a squeeze before releasing him. "Go join my brother in the card room for some time, then go home, please. It sounds like you've had an exhausting night."

"I'm going to check on Sarah first, and then I will. Thank you, Lady Charlotte."

He bowed to his friend and kissed her extended hand.

She curtseyed and moved off to where he assumed Sarah's mother must be mingling among the ladies.

Oliver stepped out into the garden again.

Sarah was waiting for him exactly where he had left her. She was pacing up and down, still wrapped in his jacket and wringing her hands in front of her ruined dress. Her face lit up as he approached, her huge smile hitting him low in the belly, forcing the air from his lungs. She accepted his cloak and wrapped it around herself with easy, elegant movements.

As soon as she was covered, she handed him back his jacket, and he slipped it back on. He was once again presentable, yet the heat from her body that had transferred into the jacket almost made him groan. He would be smelling her subtle perfume all night now, and it would torment his dreams, he was sure.

Sarah gestured helplessly to herself and looked up at him with wide, beautiful eyes.

"Oliver, what am I going to do about my mother? She's still inside, and I can't go in."

"I've just discreetly spoken with Lady Charlotte who will fetch your mother, and she will meet you at the side entrance where my carriage awaits you. She will tell them that you have come down with a sudden headache, and no one will be the wiser." Oliver paused. How did one ask about the virtue of a maiden? Did he have the right? Would she even understand what he wanted to know? "Sarah, I have to ask, did he... ah..."

She stared at him a moment, then dipped her head to avoid his gaze.

"He didn't force me, if that is what you want to know," Sarah told him in a quiet voice. "I scratched his eyes and ran, before..."

"Oh, thank God."

Her head shot up at his words, and she beamed at him. Her eyes shone, and her whole face seemed to grin, not just her lips. Oliver's heart melted. He'd never seen a smile so wondrous.

"Oliver, I know I shouldn't ask you this, considering the encounter we've had, but... I suppose it's the only time I'd ever have the courage." She bit her lip again, and although it was as seductive a move as anything Oliver had ever seen, he was cautious of what she was about to ask.

"Of course, my lady. What is it you wish to know?" Oliver added a formal bow to his question.

She fluttered her hands and bit her lip.

"I want... oh, bother." Sarah looked from side to side and twisted her hands in front of her.

Oliver attempted a reassuring smile, trying not to imagine what she would ask of him. Did she need money? Help in society? Had she worked out who he was and wanted to enjoy the privileges his rank may afford her?

"It's all right, ask me."

She was wringing his white handkerchief in her hands now.

"It's not a question, more... a request."

Oliver frowned. The problems she may be facing piled up inside his head. Did she need somewhere to stay, perhaps?

"Would you kiss me?" Sarah's words came out in a rush.

His mouth dropped open. Surely, he'd misheard her. There was no possible way someone who had gone through what she had obviously been through tonight, would ask for such a thing. Was there?

"I'm not sure I heard you correctly, Sarah." His tone was light, but his heart thumped against his ribcage in acknowledgment of the truth. A marriageable virgin was asking him for a kiss. As an unmarried gentleman of the ton—and a duke, to make matters worse—he should run for the safety of his estate.

She blushed at his words, pink flushing from the place the cloak met her neck, all the way up to the roots of her golden hair.

That blush affected Oliver more than the tears, and something inside him shifted. A blush could not be faked and showed a real depth of emotion that had been lacking in every woman Oliver had ever met. Genuine warmth, an ability to forge past her fears and ask for something she wanted. He admired that.

"I know I must look an absolute mess, but I cannot have tonight's experience be my only experience of intimacy between a man and a woman. Would you please help me to forget? Help me to make a new and more pleasant memory?" She all but whispered the last part of the sentence.

Oliver's tenuous grip on control slipped. Before he'd made the decision to move, he was already cupping her face with both hands and bringing his lips down onto hers.

He wanted to moan at the delicious feel of her soft lips beneath his, but he swallowed the sound down. She was like touching the finest silk and drinking the most expensive port. Soft, warm, intoxicating. It was a heady feeling indeed.

Feather light.

Sarah may have asked for a kiss, but he could tell she was an innocent. He was not, and his mind was already conjuring up images of kissing her in places much less decent than her lips. His body tightened in response to his thoughts as his loins pulsed with need.

Using every last drop of control in his body, Oliver stepped back from the sweetest lips he had ever kissed, and Sarah almost toppled forward.

He dropped his hands down to his sides, his lips and hands tingling from the contact with her skin.

"Thank you," Sarah whispered, lifting her hand and running her fingertips over her swollen mouth. A look of awe and wonder washed over her face.

He cleared his throat, his mind still abuzz with sensation.

Ducking her head shyly she added, "That was what my first kiss should have been."

His eyebrows rose high on his forehead. First kiss? He'd never kissed a virgin before; had never understood the allure some men found in them. But looking at Sarah's beautiful face, knowing he was the first person she had happily been touched by, pleased him more than he expected.

"My carriage will be here any moment, and it will take you around to the front of the house where your mother will be waiting. It will take you both home from there."

It was a relief to give her the instructions, his overwhelming thoughts confusing him. He didn't want to leave her and couldn't understand why. He knew it was better to sever their ties sooner rather than later, and yet knowing something and wanting to do it were two different things.

His carriage pulled up outside the gate, bearing the crest of the Lincolns.

"Oh, is that a ducal crest?" Sarah's voice sounded stunned.

"Yes, my brother." The unintentional lie left Oliver's mouth and he grimaced.

He often still forgot that he was now the Lincoln heir and his father and brother were both gone. Easy to do, considering he had spent five and twenty years in one situation and only twelve months in the other.

Before he could correct his mistake, she was dancing happily on the spot in front of him.

"Thank you so much, Oliver, for everything you have done for me. I have no idea how I could have managed without you."

She held out her hand to him, and he automatically picked it up. Instead of allowing him to kiss her fingers as was proper, Sarah bowed down, turned his hand over and pressed her soft, warm lips to his palm instead.

Shocked into immovability, the beat of his heart was the only thing he could hear. Last week he had lain with an experienced woman, and yet the feel of Sarah's lips on his gloved hand seemed more intimate, and oddly more arousing, than anything he had experienced before.

"Go." His throat tightened on the word.

With one more backwards glance at him, Sarah tucked Oliver's cloak around her body and slipped into the carriage.

He took a deep breath of cold night air and exhaled slowly. His body hurt as though he'd been in a fight and come out the loser. His arms and legs ached, and although he would have loved to head straight home, he had to wait for his carriage to come back.

He headed back into the ballroom, inclined his head at Charlotte, who was watching him carefully, turned on his heel and headed toward the male-only den. While he waited for his carriage, he could mentally plot all the different ways he would love to destroy Patrick Millington.

Chapter Three

Sarah waited with bated breath in the carriage outside the Dunford's front entrance. When her mother finally climbed into the carriage, she took one look at Sarah and her brows dipped down in a frown. She quickly pulled Sarah onto the seat next to her.

"Lay your head on my shoulder, Sarah, and we will discuss this when we get home."

Sarah nodded with gratitude and let her head fall onto her mother's shoulder, the night's events racing through her mind as the carriage drove through the London streets.

When they finally arrived at their rented townhouse, her mother helped Sarah inside and upstairs to her bedchamber, then excused herself to call for their servants and arrange a hot bath for Sarah.

"I will change into my nightgown, dear, and then I will return to help you."

"A bath sounds very... sensible. Thank you, Mama."

~

IF THE SERVANTS minded the timing of the request, then no one said anything as they filled the copper tub to brimming with hot water.

Sarah dismissed them soon after, and as soon as they left, she removed the concealing cloak and stripped herself of her gown. She almost cried as she looked at herself properly in the light. Her body was bruised and cut, and her ruined gown unsalvageable.

She slipped into the steaming bath, the horrors of the night slowly washing away.

Her mother stepped into her room not ten minutes later and stood next to the tub. Her chin lifted and worry lines marred her forehead. She appeared to prepare herself for the worst. "Sarah, now tell me. What happened to you tonight?"

Well, quite simply... "I was attacked."

Her mother's eyebrows rose so high on her forehead it made her look quite silly. She sank onto the bed with one hand at her throat as she stared at Sarah's ruined gown.

An evening gown, Sarah knew, that they had saved for years to pay for. Sarah was only getting one season. It was all her family could afford and destroying her prettiest ball gown wasn't a good beginning.

"Tell me what happened," her mother demanded, as the colour drained from her face.

Sarah related what had befallen her, right up to the point that Oliver had put her in his carriage. She left out Oliver's kiss at the end of the night. Her mother didn't need to know everything, and that was a secret she wished to hold close to her heart.

"And you have no idea who this 'Oliver' is? Are you sure he can be trusted not to talk about what happened tonight?"

Her mother was wringing her hands as she often did when she was nervous. Sarah sighed, knowing her mother could fret until she had a headache, but what was done was done.

"I don't know who he was, Mama, but he seemed to be a gentleman. Unlike the other one." She scowled. "Oliver helped me find you and lent us his carriage to take us home. Surely, he wouldn't do that unless he had a kind heart. He was the brother of a duke, I think." She couldn't remember all the details. Everything around the time of Oliver's kiss seemed to be a little fuzzy.

"You think?" Her mother all but screeched.

Sarah grimaced. Whether or not her rescuer was a brother to a duke was hardly a detail that one should forget.

"Mama, I'm sorry, I'm still a little shaken up."

"Of course!" Her mother jumped up and reached out to her, concern written in her blue eyes. Sarah took her mother's hand and squeezed. "Don't be sorry, Sarah. I'm sorry. I shouldn't have reacted like that, but you know if someone finds out, you'll never make the match we were hoping for you." Her mother accompanied her words with a reluctant shrug. "You say Millington was trying to... ah... undo his breeches?" Her mother turned beet-red as she asked the question.

"Yes, Mama. That is how I managed to get away from him—because he had to let go of me for a minute." Sarah spoke in a matter-of-fact tone. She was trying not to be overly emotional about it, even though she was still in shock and could not believe that a man had tried to force her to couple with him.

"And... you know what he was trying to do?" Her mother looked down at the carpet on the floor. Was her mother wanting to talk about this *now*?

Now Sarah's cheeks heated.

"Yes, Mama." She had a few married friends at home in Somerset, and she had coaxed the bare facts from them. She knew he had wanted to put that male part of himself in her female parts.

Her mother's head lifted, a mixture of alarm and surprise showing on her once beautiful face. "How?"

Sarah shrugged, washing her breasts for the hundredth time that night. They still felt unclean. "I asked Mary for some of the details." Mary was one of her married friends and quite a gossip. "And Mama, I have to say, it sounds horrible. Do I have to do that when I marry?"

This time, her mother blushed so dark that Sarah was afraid she had finally rendered her mother mute.

Alas, no such luck.

"Time for our tête-à-tête, then." Her mother sat down on the bed again and Sarah sank lower into the still-warm water, giving her mother her full attention. "It does sound horrible when described, I suppose, but it is how

God designed us to make children. Therefore, it should be a natural thing between a husband and his wife."

Really? She didn't think so.

"But doesn't it hurt, Mama?"

Sarah thought back to her conversation with her friend, Mary. She didn't say it had hurt, but the look on Mary's face had not inspired confidence.

Mrs. Collins blushed again, and Sarah smiled up at her. Goodness, her mother was almost forty. Sarah would have thought that she had outgrown blushes by now.

"It does to begin with, because your body will not be used to it. But if your husband is careful with you, and loves you, it can be quite... ah... enjoyable after a while." At this last revelation, her mother dropped her gaze to her hands.

Sarah's almost sputtered. *Enjoyable?* She reminded herself that her mother had more knowledge on the subject than she, so instead of stating his disbelief, she digested this new information carefully. Thinking of her future spouse, she could only picture one man. If Oliver were her husband, he would be careful, she knew. And if her mother was correct, then the experience's pleasure mostly depended on the man.

"Then we'll have to choose well, Mama," Sarah finally said with a smile. She wanted to finish the awkward conversation, more for her mother's sake than her own.

"I'll leave you then, Sarah. Take rest and sleep well. You are safe, and that is the main thing."

"Yes, Mama. Thank you, and goodnight."

The door shut with a soft click and she stood up carefully, shivering as the water ran down her body and the cold air hit her skin. She should have asked one of the servants to light the fire in her chambers.

She stepped out of the tub, dried herself with the towel left by the servants and put on her nightgown.

Despite worrying she would not be able to fall asleep, Sarah slept all night long and well into the following day, her head filled with the strangest dreams.

~

WHAT DID she want from her life and the person with whom she might share it? What sort of man did she want to marry? Which man did she have to marry to give her siblings a future?

Dressing for another ball the following evening caused excited butterflies to flutter around Sarah's belly. Her lady's maid coaxed her naturally curly hair into the ringlets that were loved by the fashionable ton and pulled her laces tight.

She had a decent bosom, neither too small nor too large. Looking down at herself, she thought they were quite pretty, as far as breasts went. Hopefully, her future husband would feel the same way.

Her gown for this evening lay on her bed, a pale pink that seemed to suit her skin tone. She knew that the lighter the skin, the better, as far as the ton was concerned. But living in Somerset meant they had many functions out of doors, and she never bothered to cover herself completely. She could only hope that her future husband wouldn't find her slightly tanned complexion a problem.

Would she see Oliver again tonight? She tried not to be too hopeful that he would attend, but she so wished to enjoy his company once more. He had said he had no desire to be married, so did that mean they would never cross paths again? Only those interested in matrimony attended balls. Once dressed, she donned a wrap to hide the scratches on her back, and pulled out her reticule. It was time to leave.

The ball was an even bigger crush than had been anticipated and within minutes of entering the heated room, Sarah found herself seeking the calm of the outdoors. Too many sweaty people in one place could not be good for the constitution, she was sure.

Her need for a wrap made her doubly warm. Her back was still visibly injured from Millington's foiled attack, so she dare not remove the wrap.

"Mama, I need some fresh air."

Her mother nodded and fluttered her fan. "Just stick to the balcony."

"Of course, Mama."

She definitely would not be venturing far this evening. Not after what had happened last time. She made her way out the open doors to breathe once again.

OLIVER SPENT two minutes in the crowded ballroom and could sense her. Sarah was here, somewhere. Walking toward the balcony, his pulse sped up, and when he stepped into the cold evening air, his breath caught in his throat at the sight of her.

All he could see was the back of her curled, blonde hair and lovely pink dress with a light wrap thrown across her shoulders. Yet his heart was hammering, and his belly swirled with unaccustomed feelings. He was excited and nervous at the same time.

Why did this beautiful young woman affect him so much? It was an uncomfortable feeling, and yet he couldn't stop himself wanting to be near her.

He swallowed and took a breath, forcing her name from his throat.

"Sarah?" Oliver called out and walked onto the balcony behind her.

She visibly jumped and whirled around to face him. Her hand came up to rest between her breasts, drawing his gaze to the plump flesh there. Arousal shot down his belly to his groin.

"Oh goodness, Oliver, you scared me." Her beautiful face transformed as she smiled up at him.

Oliver blinked. He felt as if he were in a dream. His brain was a bit sluggish in wonder, like he'd just consumed a bottle of port.

She was breath-taking. Why had he thought she was only pretty? Flawless skin, glorious golden hair and the most kissable lips he had ever had the good fortune to taste.

She didn't seem to notice his discomfort because she put her hand on his elbow and pulled him further away from the ballroom. It was the only place he wanted to be—away from everyone else, and closer to her.

"I wasn't sure if I'd see you tonight. You said you're not on the marriage mart." She laughed as though it were a joke, but Oliver heard the question behind the statement.

He had struggled with himself for hours over the issue of whether or not to seek her out tonight. He had chosen the lesser of two evils. He could deal with the torture of seeing her again, even though she was off-limits to him, as long as she was healthy and well. To worry that she wasn't all right was a torment he wasn't able to endure.

"I wasn't planning on it, to be honest, but I needed to make sure you were feeling a little better after your dreadful experience last night."

If only she weren't so beautiful. It would make this so much easier. Less personal.

Oliver only had a few more years of freedom until he would be forced to marry a lady to produce an heir to the dukedom. He shuddered at the thought. However, he had always planned to marry someone he wanted, someone he cared for.

But since he had inherited the title, his new responsibility as the duke and being the only one left of his father's line meant he was obliged to marry someone who would be a proper duchess. Someone who had the appropriate training and breeding for the position. Oliver's back teeth ground together at the thought. When had he started thinking about the fairer sex as though they were horses?

Sarah flushed prettily, the blood giving her cheeks a healthy tinge that made her glow all the more.

"Thank you, I really do appreciate your concern."

She lifted her gaze to his and Oliver had to fight the urge to pull her into his arms for a real kiss. That light touch of his mouth on hers from the night before had only whet his appetite for more of her. He had thought of little else and now that she was so close, he ached for another taste.

"It was no bother at all." He patted her hand lightly, striving for a paternal type of reassurance and removed her small hand from his arm. He turned his back on the gardens and leaned against the banister at the end of the balcony.

"Since we have already discussed my lack of interest in a marriage partner, tell me, is there any gentleman at whom you have been looking?" He gestured toward the ballroom and watched her carefully.

It had been a long time since he'd been so comfortable to be himself with another person. To be this comfortable with a woman to whom he was attracted, well, that had never happened before!

"After the other night, I'm not sure I trust my instincts."

She smiled sadly and Oliver clenched his hands into fists at his side.

Damn Patrick Millington.

"Well, tell me what you're looking for and perhaps I can recommend someone for you." The words were out of his mouth before he even thought to halt them. He was stupid and a glutton for punishment, it would seem.

She smiled at that, although the smile didn't quite reach her eyes.

"I need someone with, well..."

"Money," he sighed, finishing her sentence for her and feeling disappointed despite himself. For once, he wanted to be wrong about a woman.

"Yes, unfortunately." Sarah sighed just as heavily as he had and leaned back against the railing beside him.

Oliver looked up from where he'd been staring at the ground, confused by her words.

Sarah had just admitted to something to which most ladies would never openly admit, yet she sounded so sad about the fact.

"Why unfortunately?" He tried to keep his tone light, curious to hear her actual opinion. He knew that as soon as she found out who he was, her candour would disappear into thin air.

"Well, I very much would like to marry for love. My parents have a wonderful marriage, and I have always hoped for a similar pairing, myself. My parents want to give me, my brother and my sister, a better chance at marrying well, but they only have money for one season. As I'm the eldest, I need to marry someone who can help my family. If I marry a penniless wastrel, my sister will never get to have a season and my baby brother will never go to Eton." She sounded like she was about to cry again, and Oliver fought the urge to wrap his arms around her. That certainly wouldn't be appropriate.

He chuckled to break the tension. Hearing Sarah's voice so forlorn made his throat ache. "Well, the answer is simple. Make sure you fall in love with someone who can support your family."

Sarah broke into a huge grin.

"I'll try," she said and then she laughed too. Hers was loud, and she chortled with her whole body. A most unladylike display, indeed, yet truly charming, Oliver decided.

A smile stretched across his face. He'd never before heard a lady laugh like that, and he didn't think he'd ever get sick of hearing the sound.

Sarah clapped one hand over her mouth to stifle the noise and the other to her trim belly, obviously trying to hold back her laughter.

"I shouldn't be so loud. People will come over to find out what we're talking about and ruin our conversation." She sighed, looking back at the ballroom full of people.

Damn. He needed to know how she felt about titles before someone stupidly told her who he was.

Chapter Four

"And what about a title? Should I introduce you to a viscount? A second son? Do you have a preference?" He tried to sound as though her answer wasn't important, but he would be a fool not to acknowledge, to himself at least, how much her reply meant to him.

She was so sweet, so deliciously naïve in so many ways. It would pain him to discover she was after a gentleman who would give her a title. He'd grown up with women like that—his mother for one. His gut twisted.

Of course, there was also his sister-in-law. She had wanted nothing more than to be the Duchess of Lincoln. She had been promised since birth to his brother, and when he had died and left her childless, all her dreams had crashed down around her.

The woman had been abominable ever since. She hounded Oliver, as did his mother. They both wanted him to marry his brother's widow, and he adamantly refused. He knew she'd been bred to be a duchess, that she was thin and young and would likely produce a suitable heir for the line. His skin crawled at the very idea.

Crossing swords with his brother was not something he would ever do. He'd already spent his life being unfavourably compared to his perfect sibling. He wouldn't allow the comparison to extend to his marriage.

Sarah laughed again, pulling him out of his reverie, and it was like stepping into a patch of sunshine after a chill. Light after the dark. She was heaven. There was no other word for it.

"Goodness, Oliver, how mercenary we sound discussing husbands in such a way. I was thinking about titles, funnily enough, as I was getting dressed tonight. I really don't want a title."

Oliver's heart stopped in his chest, his ribs squeezing tight. That wasn't what he had expected her to say. He should have felt relief, knowing that she wasn't one of the ladies he loathed. But for some reason he didn't feel relieved in the slightest.

"I don't have the bloodline to attract a title," she continued, oblivious to his distress. "And I don't have a dowry for a second son to enjoy, so I suppose I was hoping for a man who would be able to look after my family, but also overlook my faults." Her eyes dropped, but before he could correct her about how few faults she had, she jumped in again.

"Oh, and I don't want him to be over forty. And I want him to be gentle."

Oliver coughed because he felt that laughing might be rude. She had the most amusing matrimonial list he had ever heard. She was the most beautiful thing he had ever seen, and she thought she should engage the attentions of a man—probably in trade from the sounds of it—who would be nice to her, but not be old. *Goodness, she was frank!*

"So? Do you know anyone who could be all those things?" she asked.

Her gaze slid over to him in a way that made his blood run first hot, then cold. Was she suggesting he put his hat in the ring? Or was she indeed asking if he knew someone good enough for her? Either way, he felt suddenly ill.

He cleared his throat and tore his eyes away from her to look out over the gardens.

She put her hand on his arm again. "I shouldn't have asked. I'm sorry, Oliver. I know you're only being kind, standing here with me."

She sounded so lost, and yet her words were clearly honest. Oliver was once again shocked into silence. She was hoping he would offer for her. Why did that make his heart lift and his chest puff with pride? She knew hardly anything about him—not his family connections, nor his occupation, nor even his last name. Certainly not his title.

But she wanted him.

He knew from the small amount of time they had spent together already, that they would suit each other well. She was kind and intelligent and as beautiful as the sun and moon combined. He'd have married her in an instant if he had met her two years earlier. If only he hadn't become the new Duke of Lincoln and it wasn't required that he should marry someone suitable for the title.

He slammed his hand into the banister, and she jumped a little. Why did this have to happen now? The unfairness of it all made him want to scream.

Sarah cleared her throat, then spoke into the awkward silence.

"Well, I don't know about you, but I shall never again venture into a garden at night." Her tone was teasing, but Oliver knew only too well how true her words were. It made him sick to his stomach that a supposed gentleman had taken advantage of her in such a way.

Just as Oliver was taking advantage of her kindness now. He had to tell her the truth about who he was.

"Sarah, I need to tell you—"

"Oh, here you are," came a familiar voice from behind them. Oliver closed his eyes briefly and said a little prayer. Hopefully, Sarah would forgive him.

Together they turned to the gentleman and lady who had interrupted their private moment. It was Lady Charlotte and her brother, Lord John Dunford.

"Miss Collins, so lovely to see you again, and looking so well," Charlotte said, curtseying politely.

Sarah swept into a low enough curtsey to pass for the king's arrival.

"Lady Charlotte, so nice to see you," Sarah returned quietly.

Oliver frowned at the change in his companion. He didn't like seeing Sarah so unnaturally timid. It didn't suit her. He wasn't sure if his familiarity with the Dunford siblings was giving her pause or if it was the fact they were one of the wealthiest and oldest families in London——next to his, of course.

John looked pointedly at Oliver.

"Oh, I'm sorry. Miss Sarah Collins, this is an old school friend of mine,

Lord John Dunford." Again, Sarah swept into an embarrassingly low curtsey and gave John a small smile.

Although John was a second son, his father's title was usually enough to intimidate the debutantes. Sarah was no exception, obviously.

"It is, indeed, an honour to make your acquaintance, my lord."

"And I, yours, Miss Collins." John swept gallantly into a low bow to match her curtsey. The corners of his friend's mouth quirked up when he spoke, and Oliver stifled the desire to push him—and Charlotte—away.

"Are you enjoying the evening?" John tilted his head politely.

"Oh, yes." She nodded; her eyes as big as a doe's. "I have never been to a house so beautiful. Except perhaps your birthday celebration last night, Lady Charlotte. I would like to thank you again for the invitation." She smiled at Charlotte and then, in turn, at John.

John's eyes widened a fraction as if in surprise. Oliver didn't like him looking at Sarah in that way—as if he found her attractive.

"We were so pleased you could come, Miss Collins," Charlotte replied.

John dropped his voice to make sure that no other person on the balcony could hear him. "I heard that my friend managed to give you a small amount of assistance that night, Miss Collins. I hope you are feeling better this evening?"

Sarah blushed deeply, her beautiful face turning the colour of one of the red roses in the gardens surrounding them. Instead of avoiding the topic, however, her gaze held firmly to John's face, and her eyes flashed with a strange expression. Oliver thought she might be embarrassed, but trying to hide it.

She was doing a gallant job of it.

"He did indeed, sir," Sarah said at last. "Although, it was no small thing. Without Oliver there that night, I'm afraid I would have been packed and on my way back to Somerset today from the horror of it all."

Sarah lifted her chin in a defiant manner and Oliver could do nothing but stare at her. She wasn't afraid to thank him publicly for his rescue and she looked so incredible when she was defending him.

"Oliver?" John asked, one eyebrow rising. Oliver silently cursed.

He'd never told Sarah his surname, and she didn't know his title. Trust John to notice. Most people called Oliver 'His Grace' or 'Lincoln'. No one except his mother and a few select friends called him Oliver.

"Oh, I'm so sorry." Sarah gasped, as if realizing her error.

She turned to Oliver and laid a hand on his arm in an intimate gesture that neither Charlotte nor John missed.

Oliver grimaced, knowing they would have something to say afterward.

"I don't know what name or title to call you by." Sarah turned, innocent eyes on him.

Oliver wanted to kick himself for not speaking up and letting her know the truth earlier.

Oh, hell!

Lady Charlotte and Lord John both burst into amused chuckles.

Sarah looked back at them, obviously startled.

He glared at his friends. They must have thought it a fantastic joke. They had found the only woman in London society who didn't know every detail about him, down to his shoe size.

"May I present His Grace, the Duke of Lincoln, formerly Oliver Lyre," John announced to Sarah, with another bow and a great flourish of his right hand.

Sarah jerked her hand back from his jacket sleeve and took a step away from him with a wounded look in her huge, violet eyes.

"I thought... you said... oh my," Sarah stuttered. She stumbled back toward the ballroom. Then she picked up her skirts and ran from the balcony.

Oliver gaped after her. What would possess her to run from him like that? He hadn't told her his title when they met, but surely it wasn't something from which to run like a scared rabbit?

Her words floated back through his mind. "I do not have the bloodline to attract a title." And he possessed one of the highest titles in London, save for royalty. He could only conclude she must be severely embarrassed she'd made such a statement. Maybe she truly did want a title and was now shocked that she had missed the opportunity? He had no idea what she was thinking, but he had to find out.

Blindly, he moved to follow her, but a strong hand wrapped around his forearm and held him in place.

"Unless you intend to marry that girl, I suggest you don't go after her," warned the voice of reason. John's brown eyes burned into his own. His hands clenched into fists.

"I just want to see if she is all right." He shook off John's arm with an abrupt flick. "I think she was embarrassed that she didn't know I was a duke."

"Well, of course, she was embarrassed. It's obvious the girl likes you, you dolt," Charlotte hissed at him. She was one of the few who could get away with calling him such a thing. "I'll check the retiring room; I'm sure that is where she would have gone."

Charlotte swept away with her regal air, and John pulled Oliver back toward the edge of the balcony. There was a crowd gathering now, their narrowed gazes making him want to leave.

The sight of a debutante running from the balcony had naturally caused a stir. Ladies didn't run, ever.

Except, his angel did. She seemed to break almost every rule he knew.

"Well?" John asked, his eyes narrowing while he crossed his arms over his chest.

"Well, what, John?" Oliver turned away from his friend and faced the trees that moments ago had been his saving grace from other embarrassing questions.

"Why didn't you tell that poor girl who you were? She looked at you like you were the devil himself just now. People will be talking about this for weeks." He gestured ominously to the crowd behind them, which seemed to be growing bigger.

"I didn't get the chance the other night, between trying to avoid being seen and smuggling her out of the party before anyone saw her." What did John want from him?

"And tonight?"

Good question.

Tonight, he had been enjoying her honest answers and beautiful face too much to let her know that he should be on the very top of her list of 'good catches'.

"I was getting to it."

John looked at him strangely, then rested his back against the balustrade.

"She's quite beautiful," John said airily, waving one hand like a dandy.

Oliver bared his teeth. The whoremonger could keep his hands off his Sarah.

John grinned. "Did you see those eyes? And those breasts! If a man ever wanted to dream up a woman, that is what she would look like." He sighed grandly.

Oliver's gut tightened and his anger exploded. He grabbed his best friend by the lapels and almost pushed him off the edge of the balcony.

"Do not talk about her like that."

His heart was pumping hard, and his hands were clenching around the black material of John's collar.

John's smile seemed forced as he answered. "Why ever not? Are you planning on marrying her, after all?" His tone was serious, though they both knew Oliver had no marital plans for the near future.

Oliver looked down at his hands, clenched in his friend's evening jacket, and hastily stepped back, letting go as he did so. "I apologise."

John quirked one eyebrow again, asking him a silent question.

"I think I'm protective of her after what happened the other night. That is all."

Oliver reached for the easiest answer. That sounded like a plausible excuse for almost doing harm to a man he had known for over thirteen years. Simply because he'd dared to admire Sarah.

You're losing your mind.

John pulled Oliver further away from the door before quietly asking, "Do you know what happened to her last night?"

"Not exactly. I didn't ask her for specific details. Her dress was torn and her back was scratched, but Sarah said she fought him off before he could... you know." He ground his teeth together.

"Fight him off? How? She's so small, she'd fit in your pocket."

John had as little respect for Patrick Millington as Oliver had, even before that night. They both knew him to be a nasty drunk and a stupid gambler, but a rapist of an innocent? They didn't think he was that bad. Or, Oliver hadn't thought so.

"Charlotte told me later that Millington had come back to the ballroom with blood around his eyes, from where she scratched him." He heard the surprise and pride in his own voice, as he imagined his little angel turning into a hellcat.

Amazing.

John gave a low whistle and shook his head. "She's got some backbone then."

"Indeed."

"Let's go back inside and see what else my dear sister has discovered."

They both headed back to the ballroom, and a feeling of dread sank into Oliver's bones. Why, oh why, had he come to a marriage mart event? He wondered if his friend John felt the same way.

Chapter Five

Sarah's heart ached as much as her throat, a sob rising and falling in her chest as she strained to stop the tears that flowed. It was ridiculous to cry over such a thing. She would get herself together in just a moment.

"What has happened, Miss Collins?"

Lady Charlotte's voice made Sarah jump, but when she looked up relief flooded her.

Charlotte locked the door to the retiring room and took the seat next to Sarah on the chaise lounge.

"I didn't know... he was a... *duke*," Sarah admitted, as Charlotte reached out and held her hand.

Sarah was aware that Charlotte was a duke's daughter, and far above her station, but at this moment, she was grateful for the kindness shown to her.

Charlotte laughed softly; the sound musical.

"So?"

"I thought he liked me." Sarah was unable to explain why she was so upset, but at least she had managed to stop crying. She dabbed at her eyes with her handkerchief and determined to be strong about the situation.

She shouldn't be so disappointed, but as the pain flowed through her, she knew she'd put more hope in making a match with Oliver than she'd admitted to herself.

"So, what's wrong with that? Can't he like you *and* be a duke?" Charlotte asked gently.

"No, he cannot." Sarah pushed herself to her feet. "You don't understand, I wasn't taught to worship a title, I was taught to fear and respect one," she blurted out.

Then she remembered to whom she was speaking, and her cheeks filled with heat.

"People like Oliver don't marry little nobodies like me," Sarah added.

Charlotte gasped, her eyes wide and her mouth open.

"Did he give you a reason to think that an offer of marriage was forthcoming?"

"No, of course not," Sarah said, embarrassed all over again. Charlotte would likely believe she was a simpleton.

"I built it up in my head after his gallant rescue the other night. I need to marry this year, and he was the first person I thought might suit. Oh, what am I saying? He told me he wasn't interested in marrying in the foreseeable future, but we get along so well, and it's so easy to talk to him."

Charlotte nodded encouragingly. "How can I help you?"

"Oh, Lady Charlotte, you have already been of so much assistance, I do not know how to thank you. Goodness me, I have been such a trouble to you." Sarah sighed and slid back onto a chair.

She had never been in trouble in her life, and she had now found herself in tears twice in two nights. What had become of her?

"I meant to ask, are you feeling better after last night? I'm afraid Patrick Millington has gotten away almost scot-free whilst you now have a reputation for being quite, shall we say, violent." A wry smile touched Charlotte's lips.

Sarah's shoulders slumped. She felt utterly exhausted and suddenly weary of London altogether. "Thank you for being honest about that. I can only imagine what he told people."

Charlotte sat beside Sarah and patted her hand. "He just said you took offence at something he said and attacked him. Which, all in all, isn't too bad."

"Considering what he did, then yes, not too bad," Sarah agreed. Then she grinned fiercely. "I did get him squarely in the eyes, that's certain."

For a moment there was silence, and then the two women burst into a fit of giggles.

"Perhaps we ought to get you home, Miss Collins." Charlotte reached out and helped to pin up a curl that had fallen loose in Sarah's mad rush from the balcony.

"Please, call me Sarah," she said, ignoring the protocol that suggested that Lady Charlotte, being of higher rank, must offer her Christian name first.

"I would love to. And you may call me Charlotte."

"Oh, no, I could not, Lady Charlotte. I just thought, considering I have soaked your beautiful dress with my tears, the least I could do was offer you the option to address me by my Christian name."

Charlotte smiled a kind, bright smile that lifted Sarah's heart.

"Sarah, please call me Charlotte. Now let's see if I can get my carriage brought around, and you can get home before anyone sees you've been crying."

Sarah focused her gaze on a mirror and saw how red and blotchy her face was. She swallowed her pride and said, "I would greatly appreciate that."

Later that night, she lay in her bed, reliving each precious moment she'd had with Oliver. There would be no more. She was resigned to marrying someone suitable—someone who would be able to help her family. She had no other option.

She would plead a head cold for a few days, adjust her expectations and start her spouse hunt again the following week.

OLIVER GLANCED around another ballroom at yet another ton event, panic gripping his gut. *Where was she?*

"She's not here," came a voice to his right.

Bloody Charlotte. She stepped in front of him, looking poised and beautiful in her gown of pink silk.

"Do you know why?" He was too worried about Sarah to feign ignorance.

Lady Charlotte smiled smugly, pausing too long for Oliver's comfort. "Of course, I do."

"Well? Are you going to tell me or do I have to drag it out of you?" Oliver demanded in a raised voice.

"Sarah decided she needed a couple of days off the circuit, but she will be attending the opera tomorrow evening, as my guest."

Charlotte said this as though she had known Sarah for years. Oliver wanted to punch his fist through a wall. Charlotte barely knew Sarah and yet she knew more about her than he did.

"But is she not here? I thought she wanted to marry as soon as possible." Oliver dropped his voice when he noticed the curious looks from the ladies around them.

"You'll have to ask her, I'm afraid." Lady Charlotte smiled again and Oliver had an overwhelming urge to wrap his hands around her smug neck.

He knew he'd made a blunder with Sarah, but did Charlotte have to make him feel worse than he already did?

"Oh, bother." Charlotte's eyes widened, and she fluttered her fan in front of her face.

Oliver turned in the direction in which she was looking.

"What's wrong?" He looked for something to justify her present stricken look, but couldn't see anything.

"Here comes your sanctimonious friend."

Oliver had never seen that particular look on Charlotte's face before. A faint blush rose in her usually pale cheeks and her eyebrows were low and tight over angry, sparkling, blue eyes.

Finally he spiedArchibald Turner, one of his oldest friends.

"Archie? What's wrong with Archie?" Oliver asked, baffled.

Charlotte could not have such a strong reaction to his quiet friend. Could she?

"He always makes me feel like I'm a tease because I have refused more than one marriage proposal. How does he even know about them?"

"Everyone knows about the men you have turned down, Charlotte." Oliver grinned. How the tables had turned.

"Well, it shouldn't be common knowledge." Charlotte was indeed scowling now, and Oliver struggled to contain his laugh.

"Archie, old boy." Oliver greeted his friend, feeling better than he had in days.

"Your Grace, Lady Charlotte." Archie bowed politely to them both, low enough to indicate their rank but also to reflect his friendship with Oliver.

Oliver scowled at his lifelong friend. "If you call me Your Grace in company again, I'll give you the cut direct."

Archie smiled at that, the expression lighting up his rather solemn face.

"Oliver, what are you doing here? I thought you had decided one ball a month was enough? And didn't you already fill your quota with Lady Charlotte's ball?" Archie nodded politely toward Charlotte, who glared back.

"I didn't realise you had attended my birthday," came Lady Charlotte's prompt reply.

"Of course, you wouldn't. I was with your brother in the card room most of the night. Why would I need to circulate the ballroom?" Archie's eyebrows rose with his question, which was a longer response than Oliver had received in years.

"Oh, I don't know. Isn't it good manners to greet the person for whose birthday the function is being held?" Charlotte's eyes were firing, and Oliver noticed with interest that so were Archie's.

How strange.

"I hadn't realised you would care if I greeted you or not, Lady Charlotte," Archie returned politely, but his words had an edge of steel that Oliver had never heard from his friend before.

"I don't," Charlotte snapped back. "I just assumed that, as a gentleman, you would have wanted to wish me a happy birthday. Given you attended my birthday event." She lifted her chin. She was breathing rather quickly too. Did she dislike Archie so much?

Archie's brown eyes were still flickering with lightning, but his face was calm and his voice polite. Oliver had always wanted the type of control Archie had. It was impressive.

"Why would I wish you happy birthday last week when your birthday isn't until tomorrow?"

Archie raised one eyebrow and Oliver could not help chuckling softly. His friend remembered everything. His brilliant memory was one of the many reasons he did so well on the stock market.

Charlotte opened her mouth to reply, but no sound came out. Archie took advantage of the rare silence to continue.

"I assure you that you will receive your customary bouquet of flowers tomorrow, which will only add to the fifty or so that I'm sure already decorate your home." The tone, again, was polite, but Oliver noticed a tightening around Archie's mouth.

Charlotte blushed furiously in acknowledgment of the truth of Archie's words.

"I do not get... I do not expect..." At a loss for words, she stopped.

Oliver smothered his laugh with a cough and covered his mouth in an attempt to hide his smile. He had never seen Charlotte bested by anyone in a conversation. She was trained by her mother, a real dragon of the ton.

"Excuse me." Lady Charlotte bobbed a shallow curtsey and turned on her heel.

Oliver shook his head and turned to his friend. "What was that about? That is the first time I have ever seen Charlotte back down from a fight."

"She probably doesn't think I'm worth fighting with." Archie's eyes followed Charlotte's retreating figure.

What had Oliver just witnessed? If he didn't know better, he would have thought Archie was interested in Charlotte, but that couldn't be. Could it? Their group of friends didn't think of her like that, having only brotherly feelings toward her.

"John tells me you have shown interest in someone. Is she here?" Archie carefully pitched his voice so that no one else could hear him.

"No, she's not. And I'm not interested in her."

He should have thought before opening his mouth.

Archie chuckled softly.

"Where is she, then?" Archie asked.

"Not here, that is for certain. Let's join John for a brandy in the card room. I'm in the mood for a night at the cards."

They retreated to the card room. Oliver didn't stop at one drink. He gambled too much and drank more than he had in years. His plans for meeting the demimondaines and staying out until the early hours of the morning were forgotten in the endless glasses of hard liquor.

John poured him into his carriage and it was the last thing Oliver remembered. He didn't remember getting home, nor his butler getting him into bed. All he remembered the next day was a pounding in his head that beat to the drum of: Where is Sarah?

Chapter Six

"Sarah, the duke's carriage has arrived." Her mother's shrill voice rang through the house.

Sarah resisted the urge to roll her eyes. Her mother was more nervous than she was, if that were possible.

"I'll be down in a moment," Sarah called out, smoothing her dress down her slim waist and noting the roundness of her full breasts, which her opera dress did nothing to disguise.

With a final check in the mirror, she descended the stairs and made her way to the front door.

"Good night, Mama." Sarah kissed her mother on the cheek, picked up her cloak and stepped outside their rented townhouse.

A coachman opened the carriage door for her, and she took a moment to admire the ducal crest before stepping inside.

"Good evening to you, Miss Collins." John nodded, as the carriage didn't allow him to stand and make his bow.

She slid into the seat next to her new friend, Charlotte.

"Good evening, Lord John, Charlotte." Sarah breathed deeply. Almost unable to get past the anxiety in her stomach, she grabbed her friend's hands.

"Oh, Charlotte, what if I do something wrong? What am I meant to do at the opera? I have never been and I'm so nervous. Please tell me everything."

Charlotte and John both laughed, making Sarah stop and bite her lip.

"You don't have to do anything other than be yourself. Walk in, watch the opera and go home again." Charlotte smiled confidently, and Sarah's stomach dropped nervously.

"But will I have to talk to anyone? Will people be able to see me?"

This time, only John laughed, but Charlotte smiled.

"Of course, people can see you. That is half the fun of the opera. Being able to see what everyone else is wearing and doing, but not having to talk to them."

"Oh."

"Is anyone else going to be there tonight, whom I know?" Sarah asked quietly, dropping her eyes so her new friends would not see the emotion in them.

"None of whom I am aware."

"Oh, that is good," Sarah said, putting on her sunniest smile.

John and Charlotte shared a glance but didn't say anything more, so Sarah rode the rest of the way happily, listening to the idle chatter and hoping that she would be noticed by her husband-to-be, whoever he may be.

WHEN THEY ARRIVED, they were personally escorted to their box by a footman and Sarah's heart fluttered in her ribcage the whole way. She had never seen anything so grand or beautiful. The velvet curtains, the view of the stage... Oh, that she had lived to see this day.

"Oh, my goodness," she cried, and rushed toward the edge of the box to take in the view.

John chuckled softly beside her.

"You shouldn't get so close to the edge, Miss Collins," he teased, putting one hand on her wrist and the other on her waist to draw her back to the safety of the first row of seats.

"Please, call me Sarah. I prefer it over Miss Collins," she told John, complimented by his attention. But she was safe in the knowledge that he wasn't pursuing her in any way.

John's hand on her waist fell away, but he held onto her hand and raised it to his lips.

"I would be delighted, Sarah." He bent at the waist and chastely kissed her gloved knuckles, making her smile.

What a lovely gentleman.

A strangled sound in the entrance of the opera box had them both turning.

Oliver stood at the entrance with a look on his face that made Sarah cower. He seemed furious. John held tightly onto her fingers when she tried to withdraw them. He drew her hand onto his arm.

"Good evening, Oliver, have you come to join our small party?" John was apparently ignoring Oliver's scowl and the tightening of his fists, but she certainly couldn't.

Sarah dug her fingers into John's arm as the flutters of panic rose inside her. He stroked her fingers reassuringly.

Oliver looked ready to murder someone. She wasn't sure why, but she knew that look was focused on John and her. He couldn't be jealous, could he?

When he didn't reply, Sarah gathered her courage and slipped her hand from John's arm and dropped into her lowest curtsey.

"Your Grace," she said, coming up so slowly that Oliver had time to walk over to her and impatiently tap his black leather boot against the carpet, before her eyes came up to his.

"You look well, considering you have been ill for a week."

Charlotte gasped, and Sarah's eyebrows rose.

Oliver continued to glower. "I apologise, Miss Collins, for my rudeness. I was just shocked to see you looking so healthy."

Sarah closed her gaping mouth and nodded slowly. Was she supposed to say something to that?

Oliver ground his teeth together. "Well?"

"Well?" she repeated, with a slight twitch in the corner of her mouth.

"Well, how are you here, looking so healthy?"

Oliver's eyes widened as though he were surprised by his own rudeness, then a muscle in his jaw jumped, indicating he was clenching his teeth again.

"I wasn't sick, Your Grace," Sarah whispered in a conspiratorial tone.

"No?" he whispered back, his face softening.

"No, I was just having a week away from the circuit. I can see why you and your counterparts rarely attend balls. They are just exhausting." Sarah let out an exaggerated sigh, and John chuckled.

"Well, it seems that the rest did you good. You are glowing tonight," said Oliver.

Sarah frowned. What was he doing now? He'd come into the box like a thundercloud, she'd chided him out of his bad mood, and now he was complimenting her?

The man appeared to be as changeable in moods as her capricious Aunt Eustacia. Her aunt was a character of extremes, and Sarah sincerely hoped that this would not be the case with Oliver, as this would make him less than pleasant company in the long term.

"Shall we sit down, Lord John? I believe the opera is about to start, and I would not want to miss any of it."

John smirked and held out his arm again.

"Shall we see you at the interval, Oliver?" John asked with a raised eyebrow.

"If you do not mind, I might stay here. My mother tends to snore through the second half."

A shiver danced along Sarah's spine. How could she relax with Oliver here in the box with them?

INTERMISSION ARRIVED and Lord John and Charlotte both made excuses to leave the box. Sarah watched Oliver carefully when they asked if she'd like to join them. He didn't move. So, right or wrong, she chose to stay.

She was a little surprised that her friends left them alone, unchaperoned, but it was an open box, people could clearly see them, and the lights were on.

The minute they were alone, Oliver moved into the empty seat beside her.

"So, tell me the real reason you stayed at home for the past week."

"Your Grace, I do not believe that topic is in the realm of polite conversation. Shall we discuss the opera or would you like to talk about the weather?" Sarah asked, with a deliberately false flutter of her eyelashes.

Sarah knew Oliver was a duke, but he was acting like one of her five-year-old cousins. He had the nerve to question her when she was the one who was owed an apology? Well, she wasn't standing for it.

Oliver's eyes narrowed at her tone.

"It's Oliver, do not 'Your Grace' me. I don't like it."

"Oh, are you sure you want to admit to the title?" A hint of anger crept into her voice, and she didn't care. Her belly tightened, and her hands clenched in her lap.

His face fell. "I should have told you when we first met. I'm sorry."

Her shoulders slumped, and the tightness receded. He seemed genuine, and it tugged at her heart.

"Why didn't you?"

"Because I only came into the title a year ago and I don't feel like a duke. It's not right. I'm not a duke. I'm a second son."

His words were soft, but she could feel the pain behind them. During her week away from the ton her mother had gossiped with the servants, who had told her of Oliver's recent rise to the position of duke.

"I'm sorry about your brother, Oliver, and your father too. How horrible for you." She placed her hand in his, the warmth of his skin passing through their gloves.

"Thank you," Oliver choked out.

"It must have been horrible to lose both of them in the same day," Sarah whispered again, looking into his eyes for the first time that evening and seeing the sorrow in the beautiful brown depths.

Oliver nodded slowly.

"My twenty-fifth birthday."

Sarah gasped and automatically lifted her arms to embrace him. What a terrible thing to have happened. Sorrow filled her heart.

She stopped herself before she touched him, noting the interested looks they were receiving from surrounding boxes.

"Come with me," she whispered, moving into the darkest corner of the booth. It was concealed from everyone and would allow her time to do what she wanted.

Oliver stood up, moving slowly up to her, a confused frown on his face.

Sarah waited until he was within the fold of darkness, then reached around his broad shoulders to embrace him.

She soon began to regret her instinctive action as Oliver held himself stiff. He needed comfort and this was how she was used to giving it. It was either too late in his life to learn how to be held, or too late in his grieving to be consoled.

Sarah pulled back and instead reached her hands up and placed them on either side of his jaw. Lifting his face to hers she whispered, "I am so sorry for your loss," and brought her lips down onto his.

As Oliver shivered beneath her touch, she knew she'd chosen the right way to let him know how she felt.

His lips were warm and soft, and she held there as long as she could. Pulling away reluctantly, she looked back into his eyes and saw a change. Something smoky and dangerous was emerging through the pain, and heat curled in her belly.

Oliver stood and pressed her up against the wall. The feeling was delicious. Her breasts pressed against his chest and her hips cradled him. Then he swooped and devoured her.

There was no other way of describing the kiss. He pressed his lips to hers in desperation, seeking not only reassurance, but a physical response. Having no resistance left, she gave everything to him.

She wrapped her arms around his neck and pressed her body closer to his until she heard him groan. His lips were coaxing and warm, and she soon felt his tongue licking her bottom lip. She pulled back, puzzled.

"Let me in," he whispered, using his right thumb to push her bottom lip softly apart from her top.

Before she could comprehend what he meant, Oliver swooped again, this time dipping his tongue into her mouth.

Sarah gasped at this intrusion, and he withdrew. She was soon drowning in his lips once again, and when she felt his tongue probing for entrance, she let him in.

Oliver abruptly pulled away from her after several moments' connection and took a step back.

"I'm sorry, I shouldn't have done that," he said, twitching at his breeches with his hand in a rather unusual way.

"Don't be sorry, I enjoyed it," Sarah admitted. "I'm sorry, I shouldn't have said that."

"No, you shouldn't have, because it makes me want to kiss you again." Oliver grinned, his eyes smouldering. "But that would be unwise. If we were caught..." He let his voice trail off.

Sarah nodded and her eyes drifted back to the stage.

"It looks like we have a few moments still. I wonder where the Dunfords are?" she mused, breathing slowly to try to bring her heart rate back to a reasonable pace.

"You mean Charlotte and Lord John?" Oliver asked a little tersely.

She smiled at him. He sounded jealous.

"It's funny, isn't it? I never expected to meet a duke's daughter, let alone be invited to attend the opera with one."

"Lady Charlotte is slightly unconventional for her class."

The pain hit her across the chest like a blow to her ribcage. "So, you don't approve of her associating with me either."

"Of course I do, and what do you mean 'either'?" Oliver asked sharply.

Sarah shrugged. She shouldn't be sharing her parents' opinions with him. However, she quite wanted to.

"My mother could not believe Lady Charlotte and I would have anything in common to speak about. She didn't think I would attract the attention of anyone of her station."

"And me?" he asked, his voice rising with an emotion she couldn't quite identify.

"What about you, Your Grace?" Sarah dropped her eyes, suddenly unable to look at him.

"Oliver," he growled. She looked up again and the heated look he was giving her sent another bolt of warmth to the spot between her legs.

"What about you, Oliver?" Sarah asked the question with the same bravery it took to step off a cliff. She hadn't a clue where she was going to land.

"What would your parents think about your association with me?" he repeated.

"They don't know. I thought I had been rescued the other night by a duke's brother. I haven't told them that he turned out to be the duke himself. I think my mother would have apoplexy."

"Why would she care?"

"She would worry that you would ruin my chances of a good marriage by telling people what happened. She's suspicious of the aristocracy. My father is the youngest son of the late Viscount Crimsbury, but my mother has never had much to do with his family. They never condescended to visit us, and my father, the Reverend James Collins, is so committed to his church that we rarely leave the area."

Oliver's face paled, then a moment later reddened, in complete contrast.

"Oh, my Lord, what am I doing?" He looked up at the ceiling and held his arms out wide.

"What do you mean, Oliver?" Sarah asked, failing to understand why he appeared to be in complete turmoil all of a sudden.

What had happened now?

~

ALL AT ONCE, the seriousness of the situation hit Oliver like a well-aimed punch to the head. Sarah did need to get married this year. She wouldn't have lied about such a thing, or what she required in a husband. He had to stop this strange obsession he had with her, starting right now.

For her sake, not for his.

He opened his mouth to explain this newfound realization when John and Charlotte burst back into the box in a shower of laughter.

"Did we miss anything interesting?" Lady Charlotte asked, with an amused twinkle in her eye.

Sarah blushed faintly at the insinuation but answered readily enough.

"Not at all. Dull conversation. The weather, the opera..." There was a mischievous glint in her eye when she looked his way and despite his best intentions, he smiled back.

"Most definitely. Very dull. How was your intermission?" he asked benignly, but inside he was grinning like a loon.

The rest of the opera passed smoothly, and Oliver didn't attempt to interfere when John and Charlotte whisked Sarah home.

He had come to a tough conclusion tonight. He could not marry her, and therefore, had to stay away from her. It didn't matter that he craved her touch and her company. She deserved more than what he could offer someone of her standing.

Although there was nothing wrong with her bloodline and her gentility, despite what she believed, they were just not quality enough to be a duchess.

He had been told since birth that he was neither needed nor wanted by his parents or family. They had their heir to a dukedom. Sarah would never survive in that world of hateful alliances and looming responsibility.

He despised it and he couldn't throw her into that world after growing up the way she had. If leaving her alone was the only way to protect her, then that is what he would do.

Chapter Seven

The following week, Oliver found himself at yet another ball, this one hosted by Rupert's mother. He stood with the hostess's son, another of his oldest friends and a spare son of the aristocracy.

He'd seen Sarah dancing but had tried his best not to care. He had a night of carousing ahead of him. As soon as Rupert had done his duty to his family, they could take their leave and pursue other, more masculine activities.

Out of the corner of his eye, Oliver saw a gentleman moving to Sarah's side. He recognized Millington's large frame and wavy blond hair at once.

That cad again. Without a word to Rupert, he strode toward Sarah.

The terror in her eyes when she saw Millington made his hands clench into fists, and the way she clasped her fan and reticule in front of her body, as though such flimsy items could shield her from the man who had abused her, made his blood boil.

Oliver's heart was hammering in his chest as he bowed in a perfunctory manner to the other gentleman. Beside him, Millington invited Sarah to dance. Thinking of nothing except protecting her, Oliver moved to her side and held out his hand.

"Miss Collins has promised the next to me, Millington."

"Y...y...yes," Sarah stammered, placing her hand quickly in his. "Please excuse me, my lord."

She bobbed a quick curtsey to Millington without letting go of Oliver's hand, and moved with him to the dance floor.

Oliver swept her into the waltz with grace and poise. He may not have liked dancing very much, but he certainly knew how to do it.

"Oh, thank you, Oliver. I didn't know how I was going to escape him." Sarah's relief at being in his arms was evident by the way she was gripping him.

"I'll talk to him."

Alarm spread across Sarah's face.

"Please, no. I don't want any trouble for you."

Oliver chuckled softly, his heart melting even more for this woman. Was she worried about him?

"I'll be discreet," he promised, enjoying the feel of her hand in his far too much.

"Thank you." The look of adoration, so bright in her eyes, made him swallow and grip her more tightly.

When the music stopped, Oliver didn't want to leave her. He put his hand around her waist and steered her toward the music room. Two elderly ladies sat on chairs, chaperoning any couple wanting to be alone.

"I love our music room at home. I'm always there with my sister," Sarah said, walking slowly around the room, admiring the different instruments on display.

"Is your family very musical?"

Another odd thing about his feelings for Sarah—he was interested in what she had to say. He could not say that about any other female, except maybe Charlotte. And that was because she made him laugh.

"Oh, very. My mother plays the piano for the church choir and my sister and I both play the piano, flute, and harp."

"That is impressive," he said.

He imagined how good she would look playing the harp, the large piece of curved wood cradled between her thighs. Biting back a curse, he turned toward the wall, hoping she wouldn't notice how his body had responded to that intriguing idea. Form-fitting breeches were not made for being with a female one desired.

Sarah laughed, the sound healthy and vigorous.

"I didn't say we played well," she joked, making Oliver smile again. "I hope I can teach my children to love music as much as I do." She looked distracted as she absently ran her fingers over a child-sized violin.

Oliver stopped short. Ladies were not meant to mention children, even when they had them. Hearing Sarah speak of her future children so casually sent up so many red flags as to make his mind look festive.

"You want children?" Oliver choked out. Not many of his friends actually wanted children. An heir, yes, but that wasn't the same thing.

"Of course. Who doesn't?" Sarah answered with a smile.

They had reached the piano now, and Oliver's cravat felt as if it was tied too tightly around his neck. He cleared his throat and leaned against the nearest instrument.

"Will you play, Sarah?" He gestured toward the pianoforte, not even sure why he had asked, but desperate to change the subject.

"Of course." Sarah moved over to the piano stool, sat down and began tinkling on the keys.

She looked up and gave Oliver the most blinding smile yet, and he took a step toward her, his breath hitching. He couldn't be feeling this strongly now, for this woman. It was painful.

A small group entered the room.

"Lincoln." One of the gentlemen greeted him with a nod.

"Miss Collins was just about to play us a tune," Oliver announced, throwing her in the deep end to see if she could handle this small group.

Sarah blushed, but kept her head high.

"Anything particular you would like to hear?" she asked brightly, glaring at Oliver behind the others' backs.

Someone named a complicated piece, and Oliver waited to see her reaction. She only smiled and turned to the relevant page.

The next ten minutes was torture. Sarah played and sang like an angel. She had a naturally sweet singing voice and she could play very well. The level of technical skill required for the piece astounded Oliver. Whoever had suggested it had been testing Sarah's ability.

In a blinding flash, Oliver saw his life ahead of him if he married Sarah. She would be a wonderful wife. She would entertain in their home. Play for their guests, love their children.

Oliver swallowed the uncomfortable lump in his throat. She would be a horrible duchess. What duchess actually spoke to her children? Sarah didn't know a thing about society. She was awkward and shy. She was a vicar's daughter, for God's sake—she would never survive in his world. He left the room with a lame excuse and a bow.

Before he called for his carriage, he managed to coax Patrick Millington into the study, alone.

"Millington, I know what happened at Lady Charlotte's ball." He opened with the bald statement, not willing to beat around the proverbial bush.

Millington's handsome face coloured unhealthily.

"We went for a walk in the garden. She misunderstood my intentions, and attacked me," he blustered.

"*She* attacked *you*?" Oliver willed his clenched fists to relax. "Is that why her dress was ripped, and her back was bleeding?" he asked through his teeth.

Oliver's temper was slipping free of his control. He never lost his temper, never. But the memories of that night were coming in hard and fast, and he was wondering who would miss Patrick Millington if he never returned home. Oliver had enough money; he could make sure the vile man stayed gone.

Millington could obviously see the internal battle Oliver was waging. Oliver watched him mentally cataloguing his answers before he opened his mouth.

"As I said, she misunderstood my intentions," he said slowly, gauging Oliver's reaction.

He smiled grimly.

"We both know that's not what happened. Perhaps it would be wise for you to leave Miss Collins alone." Oliver gave Millington a stare imbued with all the power the Lincoln name had behind it.

Millington's eyes flashed rebelliously, and he opened his mouth to say something obstinate.

Instead of waiting for him to speak, Oliver ploughed his fist into Millington's stomach with as much force as he could muster at short range.

Patrick Millington gasped like a landed fish and fell backward onto his arse, clutching his belly.

"Leave her alone, or I will ruin you." Pleasure radiated through Oliver's body as he glared down at the man who would have raped Sarah. Millington lay on the floor, gasping for air.

With one more ducal glance at his fallen nemesis, he let himself out of the study, and out of Sarah's life.

~

OLIVER MANAGED to avoid all ton events for the next fortnight. He visited his club every day and met his friends at night. He did everything possible to make it appear as though nothing was wrong.

He had no interest in any of the high-priced brothels he had frequented in the past, and even less in finding a permanent mistress. Both situations repulsed him, and he was ignoring the reason why.

He was sitting at his club with a drink in hand when Rupert walked in.

"Lyre!" his old friend greeted him, blue eyes bright and shrewd, glowing beneath almost black brows.

Oliver smiled up at his friend, letting his usual facade of indifference wash away. He loved that Rupert never greeted him with his new title.

"Rupert, how are you doing this uninteresting Wednesday?" Oliver pushed out a chair in clear invitation.

Rupert grinned and called over a footman to order a port.

"I have been catching up on the latest gossip. It looks as though another of our school friends is doing the pretty. We can't keep our heads out of that noose it seems." Rupert shook his head in resignation of the fate that awaited them all.

Rupert, although also a second son, had been made his brother's heir. He'd have to marry and produce an heir of his own, but he was putting off the task as long as possible, instead bedding every married woman in sight.

"Oh, who?" Oliver asked, interested for once.

"Jamie McTavish, and he's set to marry one of our ladies."

Oliver sat up and moved forward in his chair. This was news, indeed.

"You jest, man? He's lowered himself to marry an Englishwoman? I'm shocked."

The footman set down a crystal decanter and Oliver poured a glass of port for himself and for Rupert.

Jamie McTavish was a good man, Scottish by blood and birth. His parents had sent him to London for schooling and the boys had teased him mercilessly for his accent. The Scot had put his fist through a few English faces and the teasing had stopped. He had a hot temper, but he loved his land and his family. Oliver admired him.

"He has a bit of a fortune too, from what I understand. So, who has he found? He didn't stoop to finding an heiress, I hope." That would definitely not fit with the picture he had of Jamie.

"No, he's about to offer for a lady of good, but lowborn family and no money," Rupert confided in hushed tones.

"Good on him, although I'm sure she makes up for it in beauty. Do you know her name?" Oliver asked the question, although it would be unlikely he knew the young lady.

"A Miss Sarah Collins." Rupert announced as Oliver was taking a sip of his port.

Oliver choked and spluttered his drink across the polished wood of the table. Air wasn't getting into his lungs properly. A moment of panic assailed him as he wheezed and slammed his hands down.

"Are you all right, man?" Rupert helpfully bashed Oliver on the back with his large fist, making his lungs seize even more.

It took several minutes for Oliver to recover his breath, and for the footmen to get the table cleaned and reset. He took several long breaths, concentrating on the flow of air into his aching lungs and attempting to calm his still-thundering heart.

"What happened? Are you sure you're all right now?"

"Yes. I'm fine. Sarah Collins, you say?"

"Yes, it seems she's quite a beauty and with more than half a brain as well."

"She has *far* more than half a brain. She has a whole brain." Oliver scowled at his friend.

Rupert's eyes flickered dangerously. "You know her?" he asked, flicking an imaginary piece of lint from his jacket sleeve in an obvious attempt to defuse the situation.

"Yes, I know her," Oliver snapped, unable to hold in the torrent of emotion pouring from him.

His heart was galloping in his chest and a hot sweat had broken out on his forehead. He took a long drink of his port—this time more carefully—and embraced the burn that slid down his throat, draining the glass before he could speak again, gasping against the alcohol's effect on his mouth.

How had she found someone so quickly? It had only been two weeks.

"I met Sarah Collins a month ago at Lady Charlotte's birthday ball. She was attacked by that animal, Millington, in the gardens. I found her and helped her to get home unnoticed." Oliver confided in his friend, his gaze darting around the room quickly to make sure no one nearby heard him.

"Are you serious? I hadn't heard anything about that." Rupert whistled low and his eyes widened.

"No, we kept it quiet for obvious reasons. She needs to marry this year."

"Well, she's found her husband, it seems. McTavish is working out a settlement before he talks to her father. Sounds like he'll have to travel to Somerset, though. The father never leaves."

"Yes, she told me," Oliver said absentmindedly.

So, the beautiful little vicar's daughter had found a decent husband all on her own. She could not have chosen better and pride fluttered in his chest.

Jamie had a small but profitable estate and enough money to look after her brother and sister if he so chose. He was also not even thirty and a nice man. Yes, she'd done well indeed. His stomach knotted at the thought, but he tried his best to ignore it.

Chapter Eight

"How well do you know her?" Rupert twirled his glass between his fingers and stared into the golden liquid as though it contained the secrets of life.

"Well enough to know she'll be a wonderful wife," Oliver admitted quietly. He couldn't say that about any other lady of his acquaintance.

"She won't care about being buried in Scotland for the rest of her life?" Rupert asked.

Oliver shook his head. No, she would not. She would be happy as long as her family was set up. She would watch over McTavish's tenants, give him children, share his bed.

A sudden vision of the big Scot covering Sarah's small but lush body with his own flashed before Oliver's eyes and he saw red. He clenched his teeth and let out a small groan as jealousy ripped through him. Before he could control his wayward emotions, the fragile crystal of the port glass shattered in his hand.

Gasping as pain sliced through his palm, he jumped up and away from the fragments of glass that splintered across the table. Rupert jumped up and they both looked down at the blood dripping from his hand.

Rupert whipped out his handkerchief and pressed it into Oliver's palm. Pain throbbed right up his arm.

Oliver's brain wasn't turning over; he couldn't drag his eyes away from the blood-soaked linen. All he could think about was Jamie and Sarah. He couldn't breathe properly.

"You are having no luck with your alcohol today," Rupert joked. "I think that may need a few stitches."

He motioned to the butler and in a few concise statements, Oliver's drinks were put on Rupert's account, and then he was being assisted into his carriage, on his way home, to be met there by the surgeon.

Oliver sat in his bedroom in his family's townhouse, alcohol dulling his senses as the surgeon stitched up his hand.

He marvelled over his response to Sarah's upcoming betrothal. He hadn't gone a day without thinking of her or a night without dreaming about her since the moment they'd met. But did that mean he had the right to interfere in her life, when he could never give her what she wanted?

When he awoke the next morning, he was in a hot sweat, amidst a nightmare. He'd dreamed of Sarah in her new life, happy and content, while he grew old and bitter with some faceless duchess by his side.

He had to do something.

~

SARAH STOOD at the entrance to the ballroom, waiting for her mother who was still handing her coat over to a footman. Tonight, she expected a proposal of marriage from Jamie McTavish, and after only two weeks of courting!

She should be elated, blissfully happy about the turn of events. After all, she had succeeded in finding a man who would not only look after her family but would hopefully be a good and kind husband to her as well.

Then why was she not waltzing around the room with happiness? She turned her face toward the wall and grimaced. She knew why. Because she missed Oliver. There was something missing in her interactions with Jamie. There wasn't any spark or excitement the way there was when she was with Oliver.

Her mother finally joined her and they were announced as they stepped into the large, opulent room. There was a quadrille in progress and the hum of conversation already surrounded the well-heated room.

"Good evening, Miss Collins."

Sarah turned to smile at the Scottish devil himself, who bowed low to her. She held her hand out to him.

"Please, call me Sarah. I told you that last night," she reminded him with a smile.

"True," he conceded with a grin.

Sarah looked into his kind blue eyes and knew that this man would be a good husband. He was handsome in an unusual way and looked as strong as an ox. She had no reason at all to deny him if he offered for her.

"But I was hoping to wait to use it at a special moment..." He let his voice trail off and her stomach lurched. "If that would be all right?"

Sarah was lightheaded all of a sudden, black spots swimming before her eyes.

"Of course," she forced out, breathless although she wasn't moving.

"You look a little pale, my dear. Would you like to sit down?"

Yes, I would love to. But first she needed a moment to compose herself.

"Thank you, Mr. McTavish, as usual you are so thoughtful. But perhaps you will excuse me as I need to find the ladies' retiring room." She smiled politely.

He seemed to like her smile and her mother had instructed her to use it as much as possible.

"Of course." He bowed again.

Sarah moved along the plush carpet of the hallway. How was she going to get through tonight feeling this unwell?

Someone came up behind her, so close she could feel the heat of the person's body. She moved to the left so the person could go around her, but instead a firm hand grabbed her under the elbow and she was steered into a room off the corridor.

What was this?

Sarah gulped and took a fast breath as panic rose in her chest.

The door closed behind her and she swung around to see if her abductor was the man of her nightmares, or her dreams.

~

"Oliver!" Sarah said, her hand fluttering at her throat. He had obviously startled her.

"I've heard that Jamie McTavish has been courting you."

He was unable to hold in his feelings any longer. He knew he should have opened the conversation with small talk or at least a greeting, but as usual he could not remain aloof when he was within touching distance of Sarah.

She blushed but didn't look away, her mouth thinning as though she was unhappy. The air around them crackled with tension and Oliver swallowed hard.

"He has."

Oliver waited for her to continue but she didn't. That was it?

"I have also heard you have entranced him so thoroughly that he is on the verge of offering you everything you want."

He sounded like a jealous idiot, but he couldn't stop the flow of venomous words falling from his mouth. He had seen her standing with the Scottish laird and had been blinded to anything except the need to pull her into him, behind him, anywhere she would be safe from all other men.

Sarah's eyes narrowed. "And pray tell, how did you come by that information when you haven't been into society since I last saw you two weeks ago?"

"I go to my gentlemen's club every day. Just because I don't go to balls designed to trap men into marriage, doesn't mean I have disappeared altogether."

Had she really forgotten about him that quickly?

Sarah's shoulders slumped a little and she sighed. "Oliver, why did you drag me in here? What is it you want?"

Oliver pulled her into his arms without another thought and claimed her mouth with his. She was soft and warm beneath him, and his hands trembled as he slid them around her back and pressed her closer. He had barely a taste of her before she was pulling away from him.

"What are you about, Your Grace?" Sarah stiffly pulled out of his arms.

"I'm sorry, I shouldn't have done that." Oliver was already breathing hard. Blood raced through his body, making his heart pound like a drum and his loins ache.

"No, you should not have," she agreed, eyeing him warily. "Oliver, I must go. If we're caught here, without a chaperone…"

She trailed off just as he had at the opera, repeating the same warning. At the time it had seemed sensible, but coming out of her mouth now it sounded like an accusation.

"Yes, I know. You wouldn't want to lose your husband before he's properly caught."

Sarah gasped and there was a sudden silence in the small room that was deafening.

Did I just say that?

"What exactly do you mean by that, Oliver?"

He took a deep breath in through his nose and stared at the blonde angel before him. She made him want to do unspeakable things to her. Starting with ripping that perfect, pale green gown from her delectable body. She couldn't become another man's wife.

"I mean exactly what I said. Getting caught in here with me would destroy your chances of marrying McTavish, and him saving your family. That is all you want, isn't it?" Oliver knew he was being vicious but couldn't control what was coming out of his mouth.

Sarah's breath caught and her eyes sparked with what appeared to be anger.

"I hadn't thought of you as cruel, Oliver. We need to leave this room. You don't want to marry me. You've told me that fact over and over again. Or are you suggesting that I should have waited for you to propose marriage?"

Panic flooded Oliver and heat flushed his cheeks. "No, I didn't mean…"

"Well, what did you mean?" Sarah demanded, crossing her arms and tapping her foot impatiently against the carpeted floor.

Damn. I should have thought this through.

"I just want to make sure you're marrying the right person," Oliver amended.

"What's wrong with Mr. McTavish?" Sarah demanded, her voice rising in volume a couple of notches.

"Nothing, he's a good man," Oliver admitted, though he was reluctant to give the man praise.

"Then what's the problem, Oliver?"

He tugged at his cravat with his hands, loosening the knot. It was too tight. How was he going to get out of this now?

"I don't want you settling for less than you deserve," Oliver admitted quietly.

"And what is that?" Sarah asked just as quietly.

"Love, or at least passion."

Sarah bit her lip and appeared thoughtful for a moment.

"I don't believe you can fall in love in just two weeks. But passion, yes, I have found that."

Pure rage filled Oliver, clawing, hot, terrible anger. Red clouded his vision as sweat droplets popped out on his upper lip.

"Passion? You've found passion with him?" He advanced on Sarah like a predator would his prey. His shoulders ached as he flexed and stretched his muscles.

Sarah nodded and Oliver growled, pulling her into his arms. The need to stake his claim on her was undeniable as his fingers wrapped around her tiny waist.

"Like the passion you have found with me?" He ducked his head and ran his lips down her smooth throat.

Sarah gasped but leaned into him. "That's not fair to say such things to me. To do such things. You don't want to marry me."

Oliver groaned against her sweet, smooth skin. "I would if I could." He pressed his lips to the spot beneath her ear and inhaled the scent of rose petals.

"I beg your pardon?" Sarah shrieked, pushing hard against his chest.

His arms held tightly around her.

"Sarah, you have no idea how much I want you," Oliver admitted, rolling his hips against her which caused his prick to harden and throb.

"You want to seduce me. You don't wish to marry me." Sarah attempted to pull away again, struggling harder, but Oliver held her tighter.

He had to make her understand.

"I would never seduce you. I would marry you in a heartbeat if I wasn't a duke."

Sarah laughed again, with so much bitterness and anger that when she tried to pull away, he had to let her go.

"What do you call this, then?" She motioned angrily to their surroundings with flicking hands. "Is this the part where you offer to make me your mistress instead? Or do you already have one, like most men of rank do?"

The jealousy in her tone and disgust at the subject was obvious in her features.

"I would never insult you with such an offer."

Sarah's eyebrows rose high in silent question.

"And, no, I don't have one." He couldn't believe she'd asked him such a question.

"Well, my lord. I'm sorry, Your Grace, from what I have learned in the past few weeks, it would be very unusual for you not to have one, and it is insulting in the extreme for you to say that you would marry me if you could."

"I'm not lying, I have never had a permanent mistress, but I am aware that most men do. And I was speaking the truth, I would marry you in an instant if I had met you two years ago."

She had to believe him. He was telling the truth.

"What's different now?"

"Everything. I'm not who I once was, and everything I was never meant to be." Oliver turned away from her.

Memories bombarded him, ice sliding over his spine and skin.

"My father once told me that I was born because society expected him to have a second son, but he had no real reason to need one. He had actually wished for a daughter the night I was born. In ten generations the dukedom has always passed from first son to first son. I am the only second son to inherit in my family, and my mother has told me all my life that I wasn't needed... nor really wanted."

"Oh, Oliver." Sarah reached out her hand and touched his shoulder, the effect like throwing a small stone into a still pond. The ripples cascaded out in increasingly large waves.

With a frustrated roar, Oliver grabbed and spun her, pinning her up against the wall. His hands landed on either side of her and he stared down into the liquid violet eyes that haunted his dreams.

"You will never know how much I burn for you. Only you."

"Show me," she whispered, placing her small hands against his chest.

Oliver moaned and swooped down for a kiss, plundering her warm mouth with his tongue, all restraint gone. His hands curved around her slight body and he moved to her breasts, kneading and stroking the soft, abundant flesh through the silk of her dress.

She was like liquid heat in his arms, pressing against him and making soft, mewling noises that made his blood boil. He slid his other hand down to her rounded bottom and pulled her snugly into him. She fit so perfectly that he couldn't help imagining how easily she'd take him into her body.

Sarah threw her arms around his neck and Oliver groaned against her lips.

He pulled back and stared down at her. He had to get closer. Lifting his arms, he reached for the ribbons on her dress. He unfastened her bodice and soon he had a plump breast free. It was creamy in the candlelight, the erect little nipple a beautiful dusky pink.

"Oliver, you shouldn't... are you sure..."

Oliver chuckled happily in his throat. She was enjoying this, he could tell. He dipped his head and licked her tight pink nipple, which caused her to gasp and arch her back for him.

Oh, yes. You beautiful girl.

He bent her over his arm and sucked the hard tip of her breast deeply into his mouth, tasting the sweetness of her skin.

Sarah shrieked and Oliver glanced up to see her flushed face contorted in pleasure.

He told her gently, "Ssh," before resuming his pleasuring of her breast.

She tasted like heaven itself. Sweet, pure and perfect. How would her very centre taste?

He was reaching down to pull up her skirt when a loud voice said, "I think I saw them come through here."

The door swung open and light filled the small dark room. Oliver turned toward the doorway and squared his shoulders, blocking Sarah's body from view.

"What the bloody hell is going on here?"

He knew that Scottish accent.

Damn.

Chapter Nine

Oliver blinked a few times and stared at the entrance to the room. Once his eyes had adjusted to the light he saw his friend John Dunford, the Scottish gentleman who wanted to marry the woman in his arms, and his sister-in-law. Lady Honoria Lyre, the Countess of Sombury, the widow of his brother and the woman who believed herself the rightful Duchess of Lincoln.

"Oliver. How could you?" gasped Honoria, though the shock in her voice was clearly put on.

"If you would allow us a minute, we will be out momentarily."

He strode forward and soundly slammed the door, cursing in three different languages. If it had only been John and his sister-in-law, they could have brazened it out, but now there was no other way. Marriage or ruin for Sarah. Oliver only hoped McTavish wouldn't call him out for this.

He pivoted on the ball of his foot to find Sarah frantically doing up her bodice with trembling hands.

"They saw... he saw... oh my..." She was babbling as she sank into a chair, her shoulders slumping in defeat. "What am I going to do?"

"You will marry me." He was unable and unwilling to see any other solution.

"Oliver, I can't marry you. We just finished discussing it before... before..." She was clearly struggling to hold herself together.

"Sarah, I respect you, I desire you, I am a duke, yes, but you are from a good family." He heard himself trying to convince her and wondered when he had changed his mind.

"But I have had no training in this. How would I even know how to be a duchess?" She was trembling now.

Good question, I have no idea. Perhaps...

"You will ask my mother, or even Lady Charlotte," he answered with a smile as the solution occurred to him. Charlotte—she had been born to it. She would help.

This seemed to give Sarah pause. She got on well with his friend and if anyone could and would help her, it would be Lady Charlotte Dunford.

"But, Oliver, I'm not sure if I could be a wife who would look the other way when you go to other women, or not care that you never came home. And I want children, lots of children..."

Oliver took a steadying breath. It was understandable that she had fears, but it still rankled his pride. He would be a good husband, unlike his father before him. He never wanted to see Sarah go through the pain he'd seen on his own mother's face in the early years of his life.

"I will be faithful, Sarah. I have never wanted a woman as I want you. I don't think that will ever change."

Sarah bit her lip and then looked up at him again. "Children?"

He had to produce an heir, but that wasn't what she was asking. She wanted to know if he wanted children. Oliver could imagine that any child of Sarah's would be loved and cherished in a way that he never had been. That knowledge made the idea of progeny much more palatable. The mental picture of Sarah large with his child made him smile.

"I want children, Sarah, as many as you want. As many as you can give me." He smiled at the thought. He would enjoy giving them to her, that was certain.

"But I don't have any connections and I have no dowry…"

Oliver laughed, bubbles of happiness filling his belly. He had never thought of how his proposal of marriage would go, but he'd never have dreamed that he'd have to talk the lady into it.

"Sarah, I don't need a dowry and I don't need you to have any connections. I just want *you*." As soon as the words were out, he realised how true they were.

He already had too much money, why did he need to marry a woman with more?

Sarah stilled and appeared to be thinking over his words as she chewed on her lush bottom lip.

Her face cleared and she stood up, smiling at him as she moved toward him. "Then we will marry."

He held out his hands to her and watched as her eyes widened.

"Oh, I forgot to ask about Beatrix and John," Sarah cried, horrified hands flying up to cover her mouth.

Oliver grinned. He loved the fact she had discussed their marriage as though it was only the two of them, without any thought to the siblings that she obviously loved, and the main reasons her parents had paid for her to attend a London Season. To land a rich husband.

He could afford to give her family anything they wanted, not just education and a season or two. Perhaps he would permanently lease her family a home in London as a wedding present.

"Your siblings can have whatever you want, Sarah. Your brother can attend Eton, your sister can have whatever dowry you think would be suitable. You may have anything you want." Oliver stared at the woman opposite him and, ignoring the fact they had people waiting for them on the other side of the door, swept her into his arms.

Sarah would be a good wife to him and a great mother to their children. She would inspire him to be a better person, and he swore to himself that he would be the best husband to her that he could be.

"Just a season for Beatrix please, Oliver. I don't want you thinking that I would ask so much from you." Sarah averted her eyes in the most adorable way.

Oliver bent his head, taking his fiancée's mouth in a deep and fiery kiss that he felt all the way to his belly.

Just as they were breaking apart, the door swung open, lighting up the dark corners of their intimate little cubby.

"What is this I hear?"

Oliver flinched and turned very slowly. That was a voice he recognized only too well. He should have known his sister-in-law wouldn't have waited patiently for him to emerge. She had run straight for his mother.

"Mother." He pulled Sarah protectively into his side, laying her hand on his arm. "May I present Miss Sarah Collins. Miss Collins has just agreed to marry me."

"You can't marry her!" cried the Dowager Duchess of Lincoln. "You're meant to marry Honoria. She is the only person with the breeding to take my position when I am gone."

Oliver sighed and mentally girded his loins.

"Mother, I will be marrying Sarah. Her father is a vicar and I believe we could persuade him to perform the ceremony within the week."

He'd been caught compromising a virgin and now would pay the ultimate price. Yet, as he waited for the disappointment to register, that his life as a bachelor had ended, that he had failed in his acquisition of a proper duchess, the feelings of loss and anger didn't come.

"The Duke of Lincoln does not get married in such a way. You must not! What will people think?" The dowager gripped her cane and slammed it into the floor. The thump resonated around them and Sarah gripped his hand tighter.

"What did you do?" Oliver's mother hissed at Sarah, turning to glare at the beautiful young woman at his side.

Sarah tried to take a step back, but Oliver held her firmly against him. Now was not the time to show any weakness.

"Sarah did nothing but gain my regard, Mother. We will marry as soon as is feasible." He heard the authority in his tone and felt a moment of pride in standing up to the matriarch of his family.

"Yes, you bloody will," growled a Scottish voice behind his mother.

Oliver bowed deeply to Jamie McTavish, his heart rate picking up.

"I owe you an apology, McTavish."

He turned his head and looked down at Sarah's beautiful face. She stared up at him, her eyes warm, her cheeks flushed with heat. He looked back at the gentleman he'd wronged. "It wasn't intentional."

"Yes, I can see that. I will see myself back to the ballroom, I think. My felicitations to you both." McTavish bowed himself out.

Oliver took one look at his mother's pinched, twisted face and decided a retreat was in order.

"We have all had an exciting night, but I believe we should retire. Mother, shall we? Miss Collins, I will call upon you at your residence in the morning." He took a step back and bowed over Sarah's arm, taking her gloved hand in his and pressing a brief kiss to her knuckles.

Sarah smiled shyly and nodded her head in thanks and agreement.

Oliver ushered his mother to their carriage and they sat in silence on the ride home.

As soon as they stepped inside their home, his mother turned on him.

"How dare you propose to that girl! You are meant to marry Honoria, as your father promised her father."

He removed his coat and allowed the footman to take his gloves and hat away.

"Mother, Honoria was promised to my brother. She married him. Father's promise and his honour are intact."

She furrowed her brow and frowned at him with all the weight and displeasure he'd felt as a child. "Honoria was promised that she would be the next Duchess of Lincoln. You must honour that. She is the only one fit to take my place. You must not marry a peasant girl."

Oliver turned toward his mother, holding onto his temper despite the burn in his gut. "Sarah is not a peasant girl." He sighed. "What do you suggest I do with Sarah then, Mother?"

"Pay her off, of course. Set her up in the cheap side of London as your mistress, if you are very fond of the girl."

"Stop, Mother, now. Sarah Collins will be my wife. I will not walk away from her, nor pay her off as though she did something wrong."

"Oliver, you cannot."

"I can. And I will. Goodnight, Mother."

For the first time in his entire life, Oliver turned and walked away. He made his way to the ducal bedchamber and undressed slowly, his hands shaking despite the heat of the room.

He could not let his mother determine his fate. Too much of his control had been taken away already. His freedom, his life as he knew it, was gone. All because of a ridiculous accident.

Sarah would be his, and together they would build a life of their own.

Chapter Ten

"Did you enjoy the wedding, my dear?"

Sarah was deep in her thoughts and jumped in her seat as her new husband spoke into the quiet of the carriage.

"I did. Thank you for letting my father conduct the service." Sarah smiled at Oliver, hoping that the contentment she was feeling showed on her face. She had never been so happy.

"I'm glad you were pleased, Sarah," he murmured, the huskiness in his voice making her belly quiver.

Only six days ago Oliver had proposed marriage, and now here she was, sitting in another ducal carriage, a gold ring on her finger and wearing the most beautiful lace gown she'd ever seen.

"I am excited to see your home."

"It is your home now too, Sarah. We have many properties, country estates, and townhouses. But this is by far my favourite. It's where I have the best childhood memories."

"Then I very much look forward to seeing it."

He gave her a gentle smile and lay his head back against the seat back. "It is six miles travel. I suggest you rest. We have an exciting few weeks ahead, with our honeymoon."

Sarah nodded and tried to do as Oliver suggested, but how could she relax with so many new things running though her mind?

Her belly tightened again, and she laid her hand against the uncomfortable feeling. She was so nervous about what was to happen next that she could barely keep her wedding breakfast down.

Oliver had the right to have her anywhere he wanted.

At any time.

Would he wait until tonight or would he want her sooner?

The glances he had been giving her since she walked into the church that morning had her body heating in embarrassing ways. Her breasts tingled and her thighs ached.

Her mother had sat her down the previous evening for the wedding night talk, and Sarah had taken the opportunity to tell her mother her greatest fear.

"Mother, I am worried that Oliver will go to other women if I do not keep him happy in the... err..." Sarah stumbled over the end of her embarrassing sentence.

"I understand." Her mother patted Sarah's knee. "I believe that the reason most men of rank have mistresses is that their wives do not enjoy their marital duties."

Sarah nodded. The idea made sense to her. Why would a man want to join his wife in her bed if she didn't want him there? She couldn't be sure if she would enjoy Oliver's bed, but if what he was doing to her when they had been interrupted was any indication, she probably would.

"So if I enjoy it, he will stay faithful?"

That seemed too simple an answer, but she was hopeful.

Her mother laughed softly. "This is such a hard conversation to have with one's daughter."

"Can you tell me what to do, Mother? What must I do to keep him faithful to me?"

Again, her mother had laughed, but at least she answered. "All men are different as all women are, but the best and the only advice I can give you is not to be detached."

"What do you mean by that?" Sarah focused on her mother's flushed face, determined not to misinterpret her advice.

"I mean," she began, turning an entirely unhealthy-looking shade of red, "that we aren't meant just to lie down and wait for them to leave once they're done. Everything they do to you, you can also do to them."

"Everything?" Sarah repeated sceptically. That didn't sound right.

"Well, not everything, obviously, but all of the touching that happens before the actual joining you can do to each other."

Sarah thought of the way Oliver had sucked at her breast. Could she do that to him? Of course, she could.

"Thank you, Mother," she had replied and got herself ready to be the best wife Oliver could have.

OLIVER PACED outside the adjoining door between their bedrooms. Had he waited long enough? Had she dismissed her maid yet?

The day had been wonderful so far. The wedding, simple and lovely. Her countenance while meeting the staff and over dinner, charming and happy. But what would happen now? Had her mother prepared her?

He huffed out a sigh and faced the door, his heart thumping against his ribs. He couldn't wait any longer. He took the three steps forward and knocked on the door. A faint giggle sounded behind the solid wood.

"Come in, Oliver." The siren call of his wife's voice made his groin ache, and he let out a low groan as he pushed open the door.

He stepped through and smiled as he surveyed the scene before him. His beautiful young wife sat in front of her dressing table. Her long, blonde hair was glistening in the firelight, a gentle smile playing on her happy face.

"What are you laughing at, darling?"

"You knocked." She giggled again.

Oliver didn't see what was funny about that.

"Well, this is your room."

"I know. Couldn't we just have one bedroom? My parents always did," Sarah asked, then blushed.

Oliver could not help staring at her. Did she want to share his bed every night? Even on nights that they couldn't make love?

"Well, let's start with two and see how we go."

It was very uncommon in his society not to have two bedchambers. In the extreme, he knew friends who only visited their wives when they needed to conceive.

Sarah stood and walked toward him. He swallowed hard. He had never seen anyone more beautiful than his wife. Her face was glowing with happiness, and her nightgown clung to her slim body, accentuating both her tiny waist and full breasts.

I'm a fortunate man.

"I want to make love to you, Sarah. Are you ready?"

He wanted her to be completely willing to make love to him, not just feel as though she needed to fulfil her 'duty'.

"Of course, I am. You're my husband, aren't you?" Sarah smiled shyly up at him, and his heart melted even more. This woman wasn't just beautiful, her heart shone like a beacon in the dark.

"Not yet," he answered throatily, barely able to recognize his own voice. She had come to him and was standing before him, brave and beautiful.

"Will you also let me make love to you?"

"What do you mean?" Oliver stared at his wife, unease fluttering in his chest.

Sarah's violet eyes were glowing in the light. Was that an indication of arousal?

"Will you teach me how to please you?" Sarah reached out and lay her hands on his chest, and tingles spread across his heart.

"Touching you and pleasing you will please me." He didn't understand what she was saying.

"Well, let's start with that, then." Sarah reached up and pressed her lips to his, tentatively moving closer to him.

Oliver's heart stuttered in his chest. His beautiful, virginal wife had just openly offered herself to him. He had to make this good for her.

He stepped closer, closing the distance between their two bodies so that her breasts pressed against his chest and her soft belly cradled his pelvis. He kissed Sarah gently, holding tight to the reins of his control as she moaned low in her throat.

One flick of her tongue across his lips and that tenuous control broke. He gathered his wife tightly against him and plundered her warm and willing mouth until his erection became painful, and adrenaline raced through his body.

Oliver pulled away from the kiss and looked down at his beautiful angel.

She was glowing brightly tonight. There was no fear, no apprehension in her eyes. Only desire and excitement in her face. He grabbed the hem of her nightdress and pulled it up over her head in one motion.

Sarah lifted her arms for him and gasped as her body was unveiled, but she didn't move to cover her naked breasts when he dropped the silk to the floor.

Oliver stopped and stared, wanting just to enjoy the first time he ever saw Sarah half-naked. Her pearlescent skin was glowing like satin in the candle-light, her dusky pink nipples already erect and pointing towards him, begging for his touch.

"You are so beautiful," Oliver whispered, bringing his right hand up to weigh her full, pert breast in his hand. Plump and delicious, his mouth watered at the sight of them. He stroked the nipple with his thumb, the flesh pebbling tighter beneath his touch and Sarah moaned softly, causing an immediate response in his body. His manhood was hardening and tightening in readiness for their night together.

Oliver swept Sarah up into his arms and placed her in the centre of the bed. His skin itched. He needed to be naked as well. He pulled his linen shirt off in seconds, removed his stockings and his boots, but faltered there. He weighed his options, then nodded, choosing to keep his breeches on to make himself last as long as possible.

Sarah gasped from the bed, and he looked up to see her kneeling in front of him on the mattress.

"You're beautiful too." She brought her hands up tentatively to caress his bare skin and sensations like none he'd ever experienced fluttered through him.

Oliver kissed her softly, his eyes sliding shut as she pressed herself closer. He pulled back and gently maneuvered them so that he lay next to her. He looked into her eyes as her hands floated over his skin like a pair of butterfly wings. Who knew that the touch of a woman's hands could feel so good?

He lay still and closed his eyes to enjoy the sensation. In a world where the only person who ever touched you was your valet, the feel of Sarah's hands on his naked skin was heaven. Oliver was so sensitive to her touch that it was terrifying. He could get far too used to it.

Sarah moved, and wet suction was applied to his nipple as she sucked it into her mouth. Sensations zinged through Oliver at the unexpected move-ment, and his eyes flew open. He gasped as he looked down and saw her with her mouth to his chest. He pulled away from her, shocked. No woman had ever done that to him.

"Where did you learn that?"

"You showed me last week," she answered, frowning at his expression. "You don't like it?"

Of course, he liked it, but that wasn't the point. He was so shocked by her move that he had considered asking her if she was as virginal as she appeared. But he was glad he hadn't. The hurt look on her face showed such disappointment, he was worried he had put her off her explorations.

"Of course, I do. I just didn't realise you would want to touch me, too."

Sarah smiled a "cat who got the cream" smile and shuffled closer. "Of course, I do. You're my husband."

And with that statement, she pushed him gently, so he lay on his back, and touched his nipples with her fingertips until they tightened into little points. She then leaned over him and sucked on one until he gasped and bucked his hips. That went straight to his groin.

Then she looked up at him and moved back, so she was laying on her side.

"You'll have to show me something else, so I know what else I can do."

Oliver grinned; how could he not? He had envisioned their lovemaking as being a quiet affair, with her laying back and letting him do as he pleased with her body. He'd heard many a story from his friends, his brother, his father. They'd all told him that whores were much better bed companions. Ladies were cold, tiresome and hated the experience.

He had never had the opportunity to compare before. He would never consort with a marriageable young lady, and the widows didn't appeal to him. So, the whores it had always been for him.

However, it seemed the fates had granted him a much better marriage than those who had come before him.

"Definitely," he growled, rolling over the top of her and swooping down for a hot kiss.

Chapter Eleven

Oliver broke away to run his lips and tongue down the smooth skin of her throat all the way to the curve of her breast. Here he took his time, nipping and lapping at the flesh around the nipple until she began writhing and moving it to the position she wanted it, into his mouth.

Oliver smiled against her skin and enjoyed both the taste of sweet skin and her moans of pleasure. His hand toyed with the soft flesh of her other breast until he turned his attention to that one. The second was just as warm, sweet and delicious.

Sarah arched her back off the bed and brought her hands up to his hair to bind him to her.

Oliver chuckled against her skin, marvelling at her wantonness. He kissed his way down her flat belly, enjoying her navel, dipping his tongue into the crevice there in imitation of what he intended to do next. He had never performed this act on any woman as it wasn't something he had wished to try with any courtesan. But his wife was responsive and beautifully honest in her passion, and he couldn't wait to taste every inch of her body.

The knowledge that she had never known another man was a much stronger aphrodisiac than he imagined. He moved back so that he was kneeling next to her, pulling the pantalettes down her slightly rounded hips.

The curls at the apex of her thighs were only a few shades darker than the blonde curls on her head. She brought her hands up to cover herself, but he grabbed them and laced his fingers with hers.

"Trust me. I would never hurt you," he soothed, watching the beginnings of a tentative fear rising in her eyes.

At his words, the tightness in her shoulders relaxed, and she opened her legs in invitation. Oliver inhaled a sharp breath, releasing her hands and rolling back into his place between her thighs.

When he slid down to the thatch of hair between her legs, Sarah sat up and grabbed his head as though to stop him. He flicked out his tongue and touched the most sensitive place he knew of. Sarah's knees came together like a vice, locking his shoulders in place, then her whole body relaxed and she dropped back onto the bed with a moan.

Oliver pushed her legs apart and stared down at her, marvelling at how pink and perfect she was. The lips were soft and open for him like a rose. He dropped his head and kissed her flesh, loving the scent of her in his nose, the taste of her sweetness on his tongue. He licked and enjoyed her body, giving Sarah as much pleasure as he could. When he lowered his head and darted his tongue out to taste her core she screamed.

"Oliver, I can't... It feels so..."

Oliver watched Sarah's body tighten, and her legs start to quiver beneath his palms. So, at the same time as he lapped at the hidden button at the top of her folds, he thrust a finger slowly inside her wet entrance. She gasped and writhed, but made no attempt to stop him as he thrust a second finger in alongside it and began moving his fingers in the rhythm his body longed to mimic.

Sarah thrashed her head from side to side, then her body jerked, a breathy moan sounding as she began to orgasm. Oliver groaned as his fingers were coated in a thicker wetness and her sheath contracted around him over and over again. Amazing.

Her body went limp, and he removed his fingers, kissing the pink, wet flesh.

"Don't fall asleep on me yet, wife," Oliver teased, his voice strained. His balls ached, begging for release.

Sarah opened her eyes and groggily attempted to sit up, but he pushed her gently down again.

"But I want to touch you too, Oliver."

"Next time." Oliver captured her lips in a kiss before she could start to worry about what he would be doing next.

He lay down between her thighs and on her, skin to skin, groin to groin. They both moaned in unison. Oliver panted, enjoying the feeling for one moment before levering himself up onto his forearms and reaching down to position himself between her thighs.

"Goodness me, Oliver, you're so very... different to me."

She ran her hands down his chest and pressed her hand against his muscles as though she'd never seen a naked man before.

And of course, he realized, she hadn't.

Oliver clenched his teeth against the urge to impale her in one thrust. Why did she have to be so desirable?

"Your mother did tell you there would be some pain the first time?" he asked through clenched teeth. He needed to hold on for another couple of moments.

"Yes," Sarah whispered, looking down between their bodies to where his prick lay against the opening to her body.

"Are you sure you'll be able to fit? I know you have done this before, but I'm not so sure..."

Oliver tried to smile but didn't quite manage it.

"We'll go slowly, trust me," he reassured her, pushing in the first inch and pausing as her body gave easily to the resistance and wrapped tightly around him.

He relaxed against her and held onto his control by his fingernails. She was so wet and tight he almost shot his seed before he had even taken her virginity. He pulled completely out of her again, and when she arched her back, he gave her another inch. His cock was screaming at him to take her, but his head begged him to take it slow.

This time, he paused and looked down at her. She was staring at him with wide eyes and a trusting smile, but he knew the hard part was yet to come.

When Oliver came up against the barrier of her innocence, he thanked God she had been telling the truth about Millington. There was something so satisfying in knowing he was the only man to share this with her.

"Thank you for marrying me," he murmured, sharing the thought he had been chanting inside his head all day.

Sarah, caught off guard, smiled up at him and relaxed her tight grip around him.

Oliver took the opportunity and plunged deep, groaning loudly as tight heat engulfed his entire shaft. Breathing deeply to hold back his release, he kissed her softly, waiting for the tension to dissolve from her muscles.

"I'm sorry," he whispered. "But it will never hurt like that again."

Sarah lifted her legs and wound them around his waist.

"That's better." She smiled up at him, and as her pelvis tilted and pulled him in deeper, he moaned in appreciation.

He began to move and the pressure built in his head like a boiling pot, his balls tightening. He wouldn't last long enough to bring her to a second climax, but he couldn't stop. He thrust slowly in and out of her trying to hurt her as little as possible, but as she moved her hips in time with his, he felt the reins on his control slip from his grasp.

He thrust heavily into her, their skin slapping together and echoing around the room. The roaring in his head matched the aching in his groin, and he cried out. His body shook and shuddered as his cock jerked inside his new wife, his heart thundering against his ribs as bliss descended over his body.

Oliver's arms shook and he let his body sink onto Sarah, his brain so foggy he could barely think. His angel stroked his hair and held him to her breast, and a contentment he'd never known before flowed through him like a tide.

He forced his body to move, and gently rolled to the side, still maintaining contact with Sarah, but removing his weight from her smaller body.

"I can't believe how amazing that felt." Oliver pressed his lips to Sarah's bare shoulder, inhaling the sweaty scent of their lovemaking. Every nerve fibre in his body was singing in rapture, having been touched and stimulated by the incredible woman still in his arms.

Oliver settled onto his back, and Sarah rolled toward him, nestling into his side and laying a hand on his belly.

"Thank you, Oliver. That was beautiful."

He kissed the top of her head and reached down to pull the blankets up to cover them.

"It was wonderful," he agreed, laughing out loud as he settled in to sleep.

He should be getting out of his wife's bed and going back to his room. But as her body pressed close and she sighed in contentment, he decided that he wanted to stay.

He had once heard his brother talk of his wedding night. The whimpers of pain and the unresponsive body of his cold, virgin wife. Oliver had feared he had been sentenced to the same life. Fate, fickle female that she was, had blessed him instead.

"I'm sorry I couldn't last longer at the end," Oliver murmured, feeling the heat of a slight blush despite himself.

Sarah laughed. "I'm glad you didn't, I would be much sorer if you kept going."

"I hurt you?" Oliver pulled back the coverlet, sitting up to examine the spot between her legs. He had tried so hard not to hurt her.

A faint stain of blood coloured her otherwise creamy thighs, and Oliver gulped at this physical evidence of what they had just done.

Sarah reached down to pull the blanket back over them both.

"Only a little, Oliver, but you said it would." She pushed him down so that he lay back again. "Thank you," she whispered once more, her eyes sliding closed and her breathing evening out.

Oliver was quick to follow her, sated to his bones in a way he had never been before. The feeling went so much deeper than the physical. There was a sense of being safe, warm and blissfully happy. They were such unusual feelings for him that he didn't stop to examine them, passing quickly into the land of dreams with the soft body of his wife pressed against him.

Chapter Twelve

For the next month, all of Sarah's dreams came true. She and her husband enjoyed each other in every way imaginable. They slept until noon, eating breakfast from trays left outside their bedroom door. They rode horseback beside each other, they walked together and shared intimacy all the time, in more interesting places than Sarah could have dreamed.

They made love in the stables at dusk, in the boat on the lake, and on his desk in his library. They spoke to each other all of the time as well. Sarah made her husband talk about his family, and then she told him about hers.

Despite her earlier fears about what sort of marriage they would have, Oliver was a kind, attentive, loving husband and her heart ached with happiness.

Oliver showed her his beautiful home, the trees he used to climb as a young boy, the places he would hide from his nanny when he didn't want to do his lessons. She was utterly enchanted with the estate she now called home. Oliver even took Sarah around to meet all of his tenants.

It was all going so well she could barely believe it.

Until the day the Dowager arrived.

The butler cursed under his breath and rushed to the front door. Sarah, passing through the entrance on her way to the parlour, frowned as he opened the ancient door and bowed deeply.

Who could it be? Obviously, not a well-liked person or the very stoic, traditional butler would never have cursed like that.

Sarah's stomach dropped when her mother-in-law stepped onto their rug.

Resisting the urge to run for cover as her legs trembled and her throat tightened, Sarah curtseyed to the Dowager Duchess of Lincoln, and her companion, the Countess of Sombury.

As she lifted her head and pushed her legs to stand once again, she tried not to flinch under the gaze of the women who were now her family. She didn't want to be unkind, but her new mother-in-law had not aged well. Her skin was very wrinkled and too pale. She had an enormous hooked nose and her hair was pulled tightly against her head.

However, she was dressed in the most beautiful of materials, and her posture was so rigid, she would pass for royalty. Good breeding was stamped all over her, and a shiver ran down Sarah's spine when her gaze connected with the cold, grey eyes of her husband's mother.

"Good morning." Despite the fact that her belly jumped with nerves, Sarah greeted the two women with a smile.

Neither of the ladies greeted her back or curtseyed in response. They looked Sarah up and down, taking in her simple morning gown, and grimaced in unison. Both of their upper lips lifted in sneers.

They then started barking orders to the servants, and within moments they were in their rooms being served.

Sarah looked at the butler, who gave her one of the most genuinely sorry looks she had ever received.

Hot tears tickled in Sarah's eyes as a myriad of feelings warred within her. Why had they arrived? She knew they didn't like her, and yet they'd left London in the middle of the Season to visit.

A strange darkness filled her tight chest, and she took a deep breath, hoping to remove some of the foreboding that settled there.

It would be fine. It had to be. She lifted her chin, nodded once to herself, and went to inform her husband that they had visitors.

~

THAT EVENING, Sarah put on her best dinner gown and made sure she was in the sitting room before everyone else. She didn't want to be accused of not being a proper hostess.

"Well, if it isn't the new Duchess of Lincoln," came the cold, nasty voice of Oliver's sister-in-law as she entered the room. Lady Honoria Lyre, Countess of Sombury.

"Lady Lyre." Sarah stood and curtseyed deeply.

The woman didn't curtsey in return, which as far as Sarah knew, was vulgar indeed. Sarah studied her, now that she was close enough to have a good look at her. Lady Lyre was twenty-one years old and quite handsome. Dark hair, green eyes, and perfect, alabaster skin. Her nose and features spoke of aristocratic breeding.

Her gown was one of the most beautiful Sarah had ever seen. Incredibly delicate and expensive lace adorned the entire bodice. Sarah's family would never have been able to afford such clothing. Looking down at her pale blue gown, Sarah felt inadequate, ugly. Vanity is a sin, she reminded herself and straightened her spine.

"I hope your carriage ride was pleasant."

The woman wrinkled her nose. "As entertaining as one expects ten miles in a carriage to be."

Well, at least that was the start of a conversation.

"Will you be staying with us for long on this visit?" Hopefully, they were merely stopping on their way to another destination.

There was something almost evil about these women. She hated even to think such a thing. Her father would be extremely upset with her, but there was no other word for the air around them.

"Visit?" Lady Lyre repeated, her eyes widening and her mouth pulling down on one side. "This is our home. We'll be staying as long as we wish. You aren't mistress here yet."

Sarah's mouth dropped open. Did she really say that?

Oliver walked into the room, accompanied by his mother. "Do close your mouth, girl. You look like a simpleton," the Dowager snapped.

"Mother!" Oliver admonished, but the woman barely broke stride.

"Shall we go in to dinner?" She grabbed Oliver's arm and steered him toward the door.

Oliver threw an apologetic look over his shoulder at her but did as his mother bade.

Sarah simply watched as her husband was dragged from the room by his mother, and she cringed. As the highest-ranking woman, and a guest, it was the correct thing for Oliver to escort his mother. However, it didn't sit well.

Dinner was a sombre affair. Any conversation that Sarah tried to make was quickly dismissed and a new, supposedly more interesting topic was introduced. Oliver did ask her questions and gave her smiles that lit up her heart, but the Dowager and Lady Honoria dominated.

They spent the night talking about society and people whom Oliver had obviously known all his life. Sarah didn't know any of them and therefore had little to add to the conversation. Which, she supposed, was the point.

That night in bed, Oliver came to her, silently, and she clung to him.

They had been so happy, cocooned at his estate. Now she had to deal with the censure of his family. They made love slowly and almost silently. Enjoying each other for every minute that they had together, they made their world exist in their bed.

～

THE NEXT DAY when she rose, Sarah barely saw her new relatives. They stayed all day abed and only came down when it was time for dinner.

"Would you mind organising for the housekeeper to speak to me after dinner please, Cosgrove?" She wanted to speak to the woman about her bedroom and the way they were cleaning her bed sheets.

Her mother-in-law stepped up next to her and took her roughly by the elbow, hauling Sarah into the sitting room like an errant child. Heat blossomed in her cheeks as she tugged her arm back.

"You do not ask Cosgrove anything, you demand he does what you want. What sort of duchess are you going to be, girl?"

"I'm sorry, Your Grace." Sarah had no idea what else to say; she didn't realise she'd been speaking to the butler so poorly.

"You should be. Haven't you learnt anything?"

"I didn't know..."

"Of course, you don't know how to talk to the servants, that is why I'm telling you. You are their mistress. You tell them what to do, and they do it. They are there to serve you."

Sarah stared at her husband's mother, her brain stumbling over the new definition of how she was meant to treat people in her employ. In their home, the servants were treated with respect and thanked for doing a good job. Her mother was proud to be a kind mistress.

"I apologise." Sarah curtseyed again, dipping her eyes away from the nasty face still grimacing at her.

"Humph."

The same routine as the night before ensued. Oliver's mother commandeered him for an escort into dinner, and then Honoria and the dowager occupied all of the conversation.

Oliver stared at her often and tried to get her attention, but the longer she sat there surrounded by their unpleasant voices, the more she wished they'd go back to London.

Halfway through the main meal of pheasant and vegetables the dowager said, "I think you should hold a dinner party, Oliver."

Sarah's head came up. Wasn't it her role to organise dinner parties and balls? Why was his mother suggesting a party now? They had barely been married five weeks. No one even knew her yet.

"It's the middle of the Season, Mother. Surely there will be no one around to attend." Oliver shot her a sideways glance, and Sarah let her eyebrows rise in surprise.

"An informal dinner for those local families who haven't travelled to London would be a perfect way to introduce your new wife to the area." The dowager nodded toward Sarah.

Sarah smiled hesitantly in return, shocked by this new side to her mother-in-law.

Oliver turned to her. "What do you think, Sarah?"

A moment of panic ensued. Sarah's heart raced inside her chest, but she resolutely clenched her hands in her lap.

"I think that would be lovely, Oliver. And if your mother would help me with a list of guests, I'm sure I can handle the rest."

The Dowager nodded, and Sarah's whole body relaxed. Perhaps this would help her mother-in-law and sister-in-law see that she truly did belong by Oliver's side.

~

OLIVER'S MOTHER presented Sarah with a guest list the following morning and then left her alone. Sarah had to assume the ages and status of the people on the list, as her mother-in-law disappeared and was not available to ask. Few had titles and due to them remaining in the country, Sarah assumed they were local gentry.

She sent out the invitations for a Saturday night dinner and planned the menu with the cook. The cook expressed concern over the simplicity of the fare, but Sarah was determined to have simple, good food and plenty of it. This English preference for small amounts of delicate, complicated French food sat badly in her stomach.

The night of the dinner arrived, and Sarah's nerves were stretched thin. Her in-laws had managed to avoid her most days in the past week. It was almost as though they were determined not to help her, although they said nothing untoward about her in front of Oliver.

Looking down at her pale blue evening gown, Sarah knew she should have ordered a new dress for the occasion. As the hostess, she was expected to be the most stunning woman in the room. She knew that both the dowager and Honoria had gowns more beautiful than the one she had on. There was no help for it, though. It was too late now.

Sarah's maid was just finishing pinning her curly hair up into a complicated arrangement on top of her head when a knock sounded at the door.

"Come in," Sarah called, before remembering herself and shutting her mouth with a clap. A duchess didn't shout.

The housekeeper herself walked in.

"The dowager sent you some jewellery, Your Grace. To wear tonight," she said, making it clear that it was only a loan.

Sarah sighed. The woman had no daughters, and Sarah was the wife to the dowager's only remaining son. To whom else would her jewels belong, after her demise? Unless, of course, Honoria did not re-marry.

She opened the case and gasped. Inside was a horrendously expensive set of emerald earrings and a matching chunky necklace. The style was antique, and the green clashed horribly with her gown, but they were charming.

Her maid clucked her tongue. "It won't look well w' yer gown, yer Grace."

"I know." Sarah handed the necklace up to her maid.

She had no choice. She was in trouble either way. She would look a fright in an ill-matching ensemble, or her mother-in-law would cut her for going against her wishes.

Sarah was tired of it all. She took a deep breath and stared at her reflection, her glistening gold wedding ring catching her eye. She was Oliver's wife, and no one could take that away from her.

Chapter Thirteen

Oliver paced the drawing room for the fifth time. Where was his wife? She had to be here before the first guests arrived and he could hear carriage wheels rolling along the cobblestones in the driveway. He lifted his hand to call for a footman when the butler announced her.

Sarah walked in, all beautiful golden skin and hair the colour of sunshine. She saw him and made her way over to him the way a compass needle points due north. A lump swelled in his throat, and he swallowed against the emotion stuck there.

She curtseyed before him and gave him a cheeky grin. "Your Grace."

"Your Grace." He bowed back, grinning at his beautiful wife. He was so lucky to have this lovely lady in his home, in his life.

He caught a green shimmer around her neck, and he narrowed his eyes on the horrible necklace around her throat. "Where did that necklace come from?"

"Your mother. She loaned it to me for the party."

Her hand came up self-consciously to rest upon the emeralds.

Oliver bit back a groan. Why hadn't he bought her something new to wear for the evening? It was her first-night hosting, and he hadn't even thought to recommend a new dress. Not that he would have ever thought of it until now; the ladies in his family bought anything they wanted. Perhaps he should have allocated her money to spend on herself every month?

Lifting his gaze from the fashion blunder, he looked into her cautious eyes and forced himself to smile.

"You look beautiful." He stepped forward and brought her knuckles to his lips, kissing her gloved hand.

"Well, that is what I like to see, Reverend. A man who knows how to treat his wife."

Oliver rolled his eyes and slowly straightened up, recognising the loud and rather obnoxious voice of the local countess.

"The Countess of Tremble and Reverend Holland," the butler announced.

Oliver stepped forward and introduced his wife to a dragon he had known his whole life.

"It is lovely to make your acquaintance." Sarah curtseyed prettily, and Oliver grimaced. Sarah needn't curtsey to anyone if she didn't want to, especially a woman beneath her in rank.

The countess smiled knowingly and gave Oliver a wink. "It is, my dear. I can see Oliver married you for your looks, but what are your connections like?"

Oh, dear God.

Sarah's chin rose valiantly. "My father is a vicar from Somerset."

The countess's humph was loud in the silent room. "Married a bit below you, didn't you?"

Oliver's spine straightened as he placed Sarah's shaking hand on his arm and drew her close.

"I don't believe so, my lady," he drawled.

The woman cackled with laughter.

Oliver's mother chose that moment to enter the room.

"Your Grace," the countess greeted the dowager with a short curtsey.

The dowager nodded back.

"You let Oliver marry someone with no connections?" the countess asked.

"My son chose his wife, not I."

Sarah flushed and Oliver bristled, pulling his wife closer to his side. He started walking toward the door before he spoke.

"If you don't like my choices, Mother, you are welcome to retire to the dowager house."

The room went silent, and he turned to his angel.

"Let us stand at the door to greet our guests, my dear."

Sarah nodded once and followed his lead. Oliver knew his mother could be very nasty indeed, but he'd seen little so far to indicate any real malice.

Even so, he was determined to protect Sarah if need be. He could only hope the rest of the night would go better.

~

THEY WERE ALL DRESSED EXQUISITELY. No simple country gentry, these people.

Some of their guests were downright rude, others just curious. There was one girl Sarah's age that she had hoped might become a friend, but she was soon informed that, "I was meant to marry His Grace; how dare he marry you?"

Sarah managed, "Oh? I thought he was supposed to marry Honoria," but at the shocked gasps around her, she was relieved that Oliver pulled her out of that conversation quickly. But the damage had been done.

They were escorted into dinner by the footmen. Sarah hadn't been told the hierarchy of her guests so had placed them evenly around the room, putting wives and husbands on opposite sides of the dinner table. She knew that most dinner parties were seated gentleman, then lady, but she thought Oliver would enjoy it more to be seated with a man on either side of him, and Sarah placed a woman on either side of her.

When everyone was seated, there was silence for a good five minutes, and Sarah drank her glass of red wine with shaking hands.

Why wasn't anyone talking? What had she done wrong already?

The first course was served, and Sarah heard one of the male guests make an encouraging remark about the serving size. Happy with one thing, at least, Sarah tried to converse with the elderly woman to her right. Unfortunately, the woman was stone deaf, and Sarah could not bring herself to shout in her ear.

The woman to her left spent the whole dinner flirting atrociously with the man opposite her, who Sarah knew wasn't her husband.

By the end of the meal, the table was loudly conversing, and Sarah was proud in the knowledge that people finally appeared to be having a good time. After their chocolate pudding dessert, that few ladies touched, Oliver called the men to the library for cigars and port, and the dowager announced that the women would retire to the sitting room.

Despite feeling completely out of her depth, Sarah kept her chin up and made a resolution to keep smiling, even if things turned ugly. Being separated from Oliver was not a good thing. She would be vulnerable to attack now.

It didn't take long.

"I cannot believe what she served us for dinner," one of the ladies hissed at her friend as Sarah entered the room.

"Good enough for the servants," came the nasty reply.

Sarah saw her mother-in-law smirking in the corner, but she didn't waver in her stride as she walked around the room. Her stomach gripped hard, making her food churn.

"Weren't you taught how to seat a table for dinner?" a rather tight-lipped woman asked her, glaring through her black spectacles.

Sarah recognised her as the wife of the man whom the woman next to her had been flirting with throughout dinner. Blood flowed into her cheeks, making her want to run. She hated how obvious her blushes were, but as the hostess, hiding in a corner wasn't an option.

"I thought it would be more interesting this way," Sarah answered honestly.

Why was she being attacked for such a simple thing? Did she have to follow all the rules laid down by society, all the time?

"Pardon me?" came a familiar voice from behind her.

Sarah shivered as a cold hand danced along her spine, and she turned to her sister-in-law.

"How is it interesting to flout every rule, and insult the hierarchy upon which the civilization of England is proudly based?"

Sarah's heart jumped up into her throat. How did one even try to answer that question?

"Stop picking on the poor girl; she's a vicar's daughter," said the Countess of Tremble, and dismissed the issue with a wave of her large hand.

Sarah stared at Honoria a moment longer, wishing she had the strength to simply tell the woman she was not welcome here. But of course, she could not do that.

"I loved the food, myself," the countess declared, and went on happily talking about the meal, the chocolate pudding in particular.

At least one person enjoyed the dinner, she thought, absurdly grateful to the countess despite her obnoxious manner.

She sat down on a settee with a cup of tea and held her tongue for the rest of the evening, afraid she would either burst into tears or shout some unruly words at those of the guests ruder than others. Eventually, she stood to say goodnight. She struggled to maintain her smile, and there was a heavy weight sitting in her belly, unlike anything she'd ever known.

She had never felt so useless in her life.

"WHAT A HORRIBLE EVENING."

Sarah shared the remark with her husband in an attempt to lighten the weight gripping her, as Oliver pulled back the blankets and climbed into the bed next to her.

"Hardly. I had more fun than I've had in ages." Oliver chuckled, reaching out to pull her into his side.

"But I did everything wrong. The seating wasn't organised properly, the food was too plain, and your mother said I was dressed like a servant." Sarah shuddered as she relived the moment the dowager pulled her aside to tell her that her dress was little better than the housekeeper's. At least it hadn't been in front of their guests.

Her mother-in-law was, quite simply, a horrible woman, as was Oliver's sister-in-law.

Oliver sighed. "Sarah, I conversed with people I never get to speak to and the food was delicious. If you didn't feel pretty enough in that gown, then we will order some new ones. Get the seamstress in the village to come to the house."

Disappointment assailed her as Oliver dismissed her concerns by offering to buy her dresses, but as Sarah stared at him, she saw nothing to alarm her. He looked drowsy and happy, as though he had spent a pleasant evening with his friends, rather than the dreadful night she had experienced. She had hated every minute of it, but if Oliver was happy, then she was resolved not to let it upset her.

Time to shift the mood to something more appropriate.

"What sort of dresses do you want me in, Oliver?"

Sarah let a small moan escape her as she stretched her body under the sheet so that he could see the mounds of her breasts and the smooth slope of her belly.

"Anything that covers this delicious body up so that no one else gets to see it."

Oliver pulled the sheet down and her nightgown up so that cool air brushed her breasts. He set his lips to one sensitive nipple and suckled greedily. Sarah moaned loudly and held the man she loved to her. Their conversation was at an end.

~

THE NEXT DAY was another round of "who can make Sarah feel bad without Oliver hearing." Her mother-in-law criticised her for wearing a dress not fitting of her station and then told Sarah she needed lessons in deportment.

Honoria went to the housekeeper and changed all the menus for the week without telling Sarah, adding several seafood dishes to which Sarah was allergic.

It was only when the housekeeper mentioned it, that Sarah became aware. She explained her allergies and the menus were amended once more.

To deal with the stress, Sarah began dusting. She always did that at home. If she had something on her mind or needed to think, then an easy, yet constructive task was always best. She was dusting one of the sitting rooms when her mother-in-law came in, dragging one of the maids by the ear.

"Look, just look at what she is doing. If you did your job right then she would not be dusting the shelves!" The dowager screamed at the poor girl, who could not have been more than sixteen.

The maid turned bright pink and promptly burst into tears. Sarah's heart squeezed tight in her chest. She was obviously the worst mistress in the world.

"I should not have been cleaning, Your Grace," Sarah apologised, blinking rapidly and trying her best not to burst into tears herself.

"No, you should not. You obviously have problems with the cleanliness of the house. Therefore, I will dismiss this maid instantly."

The maid in question fell to her knees, sobbing into her white pinafore.

Don't you dare!

She could not be the reason this poor girl lost her job. Goodness knows what fate she would have without it.

"No, please do not do that, Your Grace. I was simply selfish and vain wanting to do it myself." She looked down at the maid on the floor. "You will not lose your job," she assured the girl.

Her mother-in-law eyed her critically, and then inhaled deeply and screamed for Oliver.

Sarah cringed at the sound, clenching her teeth as her anger rose.

"Yes, Mother," came a weary voice from the doorway.

"Your wife has been *dusting*."

Oliver's gaze swung to her and narrowed onto the feather duster in her hand.

"And what is the problem, Mother?"

Thank you!

"She is a *duchess*. What will people think when they find out that she takes chores away from the servants?"

Oliver stiffened. Embarrassment sliced through her and tears threatened. No. She would not cry. She was determined not to cry in front of this hideous woman.

"Sarah isn't used to having the servant numbers that we have, Mother. You can't expect her to know what to do in every situation."

Sarah's tears melted away as her anger grew. Was what she was doing so wrong? This was *their* home, not his mother's any longer. She belonged in the Dowager House. Yet the manners Sarah had been brought up with made her refrain from saying so out loud.

His mother continued. "This is my home, Oliver, and I will not have her undermining me. This maid is to be let go immediately."

"No," Sarah said stubbornly. "She is not to be let go."

Oliver groaned and motioned for the girl to leave the room. "Mother, this is not a subject for me. Sarah is the mistress here now, and I am sure you will find her very agreeable. I need to get back to the library. Can you and Sarah sort this out, please?"

His mother nodded, triumphant, obviously assuming she would now get her way. Sarah sagged, exhausted at dealing with this on a constant basis.

Plus, she was annoyed with Oliver, if she was honest with herself. How could her husband not stand up for her? She sent him a glare as he bowed himself out of the room. Sarah received another nasty look from her mother-in-law before she too, left Sarah alone.

Sarah immediately went to the housekeeper and asked for that particular maid to attend her in her rooms that evening. When the maid arrived that night, she was immensely relieved. At least she had won that round, and the guilt of the maid's unemployment wasn't hanging over Sarah's head. Having two ladies' maids came in quite handy, too.

Sarah put a hand to her chest to take a deep breath. She was constantly out of breath these days and often felt faint. She needed to sort things out with Oliver, and find a solution for the dowager—and Honoria too—as quickly as possible. Her health was beginning to suffer.

That night, Oliver joined Sarah in her bed as he always did, and yet there was something different about their encounter. They came together almost violently, each seeking reassurance that they were there for each other.

Sarah clung to her husband, revelling in the deep thrusts of his body. Knowing that in this, at least, she was a perfect wife and he a perfect husband. She was helpless not to respond and came apart loudly in his arms, calling forth his own release within moments. They lay beside each other panting and together they drifted into sleep, hands linked.

~

Over the next week things got steadily worse. The dowager began to criticize Sarah's piano playing, so Sarah stopped playing the instrument that had given her great joy since she could walk.

Honoria told her that her embroidery was little better than a child's, so she stopped her needlework. She didn't know where to turn, and when she tried to speak to Oliver about it, he brushed it off with the cavalier statement, "That is just the way they are."

Sarah felt alone, and the constant berating caused her to begin doubting herself in everything. She started to believe that she was completely inadequate in all areas of her life, and she didn't know how to fix any of it. Never had she been so close to despair. She wanted her parents—her mother in particular. Who better to guide her out of this pit of blackness? But she was frightened to send her mother a letter that could be intercepted by Oliver's mother or sister-in-law. She couldn't bear to put her mother in danger of their hideous abuse.

Everywhere Sarah looked were reminders of the difference between herself and her husband's way of life. The house, the food, the servants, his family.

Sarah was close to breaking point with no way of turning back.

~

Oliver wasn't oblivious to Sarah's pain. He knew, or had a fair idea, how bad it was getting for her. He had heard his mother criticise Sarah for her piano playing through an open door and hadn't said anything.

He knew that Honoria went over Sarah's head when it came to the house-keeping. Never in public conversation, and never in front of him. But his valet kept him informed.

Initially he thought it would make things worse if he stepped in. He hoped things would naturally settle, or that the women would find a new rhythm with living together.

But then his mother began to ridicule him too—as she had done all his life, but she seemed to step up her taunts to an intolerable level. Telling him his coat wasn't the latest style or that his speech wasn't eloquent enough, or that his father would be ashamed of the state of the grounds and the way the tenants were not being looked after.

She stated bluntly one day that he was a dreadful duke and it was a shame his brother was the one who had died alongside their father.

He'd erected armour around his feelings for most of his life, but the implication that she'd have preferred him dead over his brother, stung.

Every day he sensed the holes in his armour getting larger as she chipped away at him.

The only solace in the whole day was when he climbed into Sarah's bed at night. There he found heaven. Sarah opened her arms and her heart and welcomed him. She never turned him away; she never said no to his needs.

Even one night when he didn't feel able to make love to her, he held her all night, and she clung tightly to him. She never reproached or criticised him.

The only thing she did was complain about how his mother and Honoria treated her. He didn't know what to do about that—either for her, or himself.

SARAH HAD HAD ENOUGH. She had been spoken down to, criticised and glared at every day for almost a month and she was at breaking point.

She loved her husband, but she couldn't keep living like this. It wasn't good for her, and it wasn't healthy for the baby she suspected was growing inside her. She hadn't had her monthly flux in the eight weeks since her wedding.

Sarah knew she needed to approach her husband and give him a chance to be the man she knew he could be.

She walked the lonely halls of his estate and found Oliver in his study, where he normally remained during the day.

"Oliver, I don't think I can stay in this house with your mother any longer."

The words came out in a rush. It had taken all day to find the courage to speak up and now that she had, she wondered why she hadn't done it a month before.

"It's her home. I can't ask her to leave." Oliver looked at her, his eyes rimmed with dark circles. He looked tired and out of sorts, but for once her heart did not soften when she saw him. Not when he refused to ask his mother to leave.

"And, Honoria..." Sarah began, unsure how she could describe her husband's sister-in-law without using a curse word. "She looks at me as though I were a rodent who had the audacity to find its way into her room."

"Surely Honoria's not that bad, Sarah. Are you not exaggerating a little? I know you didn't grow up with ladies like Honoria and my mother, but in my experience they are not unusual. Can you not find a way to cope better with their disagreeable natures?"

Cope better? Me?

Anger rose in her chest. "Why is she still living here?" She placed her hands on hips as she glared at her husband.

"Because I promised her she would always have a place to live within our family. I didn't have much choice. My brother didn't leave her enough money to afford her own home. Also, she's good company for my mother."

"But I'm your *wife*," Sarah argued. *She* was supposed to be the one his mother wanted to keep her company.

"Of course, you are."

"Then why do they both hate me so much? I knew they weren't happy that you had married so far beneath your station, but I never thought they would be so horrible to me." Sarah allowed every ounce of hurt to show in her face and voice, hoping to reach Oliver.

Instead, he seemed to shrink further into himself.

"Sarah, you're exaggerating, and it is unbecoming, especially in a duchess."

"I'm not exaggerating. They don't think I'm good enough for you."

Oliver remained silent.

"Oliver!" She yelled His name, furious that he was not automatically taking her side.

"Yes?"

"Tell me the truth. Do *you* think I'm good enough to be your wife?"

"Of course, you are. You are the only one I've ever wanted." The sadness in his voice just about broke her heart.

"Then why can't you see that your mother and your brother's wife are totally disrespectful toward me?"

"What can I say, Sarah? Nothing I am telling you is making you feel better. Tell me what you want me to say?"

"Tell me why they don't like me," She needed an answer to that question, but she was also desperate to reach Oliver on a level that wasn't just physical.

Oliver sighed, the sound long and tired.

"Because my mother was raised to believe only people who were born with titles have any value, and my sister-in-law not only feels the same way, but she's also jealous that I chose you over her."

"What? She wanted you to marry *her*?"

That is just ludicrous!

"It's not that uncommon. She was raised to be the Duchess of Lincoln. She was betrothed to my brother from birth."

Sarah inhaled sharply, fear suffocating her. "Did you *want* to marry her?"

"Of course not. If I had, the wedding would have taken place the week we were out of mourning." Oliver sounded angry that she had even asked.

"Oh. Good." Sarah exhaled, unable to keep her relief from showing.

"Not that she wouldn't have been a perfect duchess, but the idea of sharing a bed with her, in the same bed that my brother had... no."

Sarah didn't hear anything except that Oliver thought that his sister-in-law would be a better duchess than her.

"So, you believe it too!" She exploded, her heart hammering in her chest as every muscle in her body grew taut. "You don't think I'm good enough to be your duchess."

Oliver opened his mouth to answer, but nothing came out.

Pain similar to a knife sliding between her ribs hit her. "*What is wrong with you, Oliver?*" She screeched the words then turned and fled, running all the way back to her bedroom, and cried until she could barely draw breath. Her maid rushed in after she had cried herself hoarse.

"You must stop, yer Grace, it is not good fer the baby."

Her maid, Sophie, applied a cold cloth to her face, and Sarah choked on a fresh wave of tears.

"How did you..." Sarah started to ask, before realising who washed her underclothes every day.

"Please don't say anything to anyone. I haven't told my husband yet," Sarah begged her. Her mother-in-law's voice taunted her in the back of her head. *A duchess does not ask, she commands.*

"Of course not, yer Grace. It is sometimes good to wait to make sure it is safe."

Sarah pressed an anxious hand to her abdomen. She could not lose her baby. It was the one thing she had been able to do that her horrible sister-in-law hadn't. Provide the dukedom with an heir.

"I think I need to sleep. Will you inform the cook and the dowager duchess that I won't be down for dinner?" Sarah lay back and closed her eyes, wishing herself far away.

"Of course, yer Grace. Could I perhaps draw you a bath before you retire?" Sophie's concern coloured her voice.

Usually, this would have soothed Sarah, knowing there was one person in her life who cared how she felt, but she was too miserable to think about it today.

"No thank you, I just need to lie here." She was so emotionally exhausted that she fell straight into a dreamless sleep.

❧

"Not even two months she's been here and already she's started thinking of herself as too important to meet with us for dinner."

Oliver heard his mother from his end of the table, and wished that the already huge table was even longer.

"Mother. Enough."

"Did you hear her directing the housekeeper to change the menus that I had already ordered for the week?" Honoria asked the dowager, disgust apparent in her voice.

Now they were both ignoring him.

"Have you heard the way she speaks to the servants? She treats them as though they are her equals!" the dowager said.

"That is because they are." The both laughed, and Oliver reached for the port decanter.

He tried once more. "You both need to give Sarah a chance. She is a beautiful lady."

The two ladies acted as though he hadn't spoken and dinner continued in this vein. Oliver drowned himself in a bottle of his best port, and his closest relations spent the evening saying horrible things about his new wife.

He spoke up several times against them, but again he was ignored.

He was so cup shot by dessert he had to have a footman help him to bed, where he slept off his intoxication alone.

Chapter Fifteen

Sarah woke partway through the night and listened, hoping to hear some movement in the room next door. For the first time since they had married, Oliver didn't join her in her bed. She was completely alone now, and it was her fault. She had destroyed the one good thing they had together by speaking her fears aloud, and now her husband wouldn't come to her.

Around dawn she fell asleep again, only to re-awaken when her maid came in to inform her that lunch would be served soon.

Sarah gasped and sat bolt upright. How could she have missed breakfast? She twisted and placed her feet on the floor, jumping out of bed. She swooned and would have fainted dead away if her quick thinking maid hadn't pushed her in the direction of the bed.

She landed with a thump on the soft mattress, black spots still swimming in her eyes. They slowly receded, and she took long, deep breaths.

"There now, yer Grace. Do not you be getting up so quickly. The last thing you need is a fall."

Sarah lay a hand to her spinning head and swallowed the bile that rose in her throat. The dizziness she usually felt had been multiplied this morning, and she was feeling very sick in the stomach, too.

"Thank you, Sophie. I am feeling quite ill. Do you think I could have some toast and tea in my room?" Sarah winced at the tone she was using to talk to her servant. Her mother-in-law would be disgusted.

Well, her mother-in-law could fall in the lake for all she cared. She had a new priority, her baby.

She wasn't willing to give up on her husband, but until her pregnancy was better established she would have to protect herself. That would mean not allowing her in-laws to cause her distress, and not upsetting herself over Oliver's withdrawal from everything.

Sophie brought in her tray of toast and tea, and Sarah sat up in her bed and nibbled on her very late breakfast. Drinking slowly and eating slower, she waited for her body to respond to the food. After eating, she had another nap.

The next time she awoke, Sarah felt more relaxed than she had in a month. The weight of the world had been lifted from her shoulders. She was pregnant. She had to get outside, get some fresh air, and avoid her toxic mother-in-law and sister-in-law at all costs.

Dressing in one of her old walking dresses, Sarah slipped out the servant's entrance with help from Sophie and the housekeeper and made her way to the stables. Walking slowly and enjoying the gentle breeze, she almost bumped into Oliver.

"Oh, Oliver, I'm sorry." Sarah stepped back from where her husband was talking to his horse. It looked like he had just gotten back from a ride. He was sweating, and his hair was windswept and unkempt. He looked so delicious Sarah's body heated, and her nipples peaked beneath her dress.

"Sarah." Oliver greeted her with a bow. "Are you all right? You look pale."

At least he still noticed what she looked like, even if it wasn't very complimentary.

"I think I stayed indoors for too long. I decided to go for a walk around the lake." Sarah gathered her courage and managed to smile invitingly at her husband. "Would you care to join me?"

Oliver hesitated. "I would love to, but I need to get back to the house to bathe in time for dinner. Perhaps tomorrow?"

Sarah nodded and glanced away, ignoring the sadness that threatened to overwhelm her.

Oliver headed back to the house, and Sarah continued on her journey. She meandered around the beautiful lake that was one of the many places Oliver had shown her in the first days they were here together.

Her cheeks heated when she passed a secluded grassy patch where he had made love to her. Pressing a hand to her belly, she wondered when they had conceived this child. Perhaps it had been that day? Perhaps it had even been their wedding night? Either way, this child had been conceived in love, and she would fight to keep it safe.

Sarah lost track of time, returning to the house when the sun was setting, and the family was assembling for dinner.

"What time do you call this?" The dowager boomed from the sitting room where they were taking pre-dinner drinks.

Sarah went to drop into an automatic curtsey but stopped herself. She was now of the same rank as her mother-in-law, and she needn't curtsey to anyone ever again. Straightening her spine, she stared into the older woman's cold, grey eyes.

"I lost track of time."

"Well, you'll never be ready in time for dinner, and you are not wearing that peasant dress in my dining room."

"Mother, stop. We'll wait for Sarah, as long as is necessary."

Sarah smiled and inclined her head. "I will wear what I wish in *my* dining room. But I've changed my mind. Please, don't wait for me. I will dine in my room."

Oliver's mouth dropped open, as did the dowager and Honoria's mouths beside him. Without a backward glance, she turned and walked up the grand staircase.

One footman was trying to suppress a smile as she walked past him and she started to giggle. What a relief it was to be able to ignore them now. She was sorry she would not be eating with Oliver, but it had to be done. For the sake of her baby, she would not subject herself to the stress of that dining room again.

❧

OLIVER COULD NOT BELIEVE what had just happened. He had been waiting anxiously for his wife to arrive, fearing the explosion from his mother that was sure to come because of Sarah's tardiness.

Instead, Sarah had refused to curtsey to his mother, a first for her, of which Oliver was intensely proud, but then she had made that comment about her dining room, and left him to have dinner alone. Well, not alone exactly, but without her, he may as well be.

"We will return to London on Friday, Oliver," his mother announced during the main course.

"Of course, Mother, I understand." He tried his best to look disappointed, but inside, he was relieved.

If they left, perhaps he and Sarah could go back to how they had been before his mother had arrived. He wanted to return to her bed, but how could he, whilst things were still so strained between them?

"All of us," his mother corrected.

"Pardon?" Oliver's eyebrows rose as he sat up straighter in his chair.

"You will join Honoria and me for the remainder of the Season." The dowager's tone brooked no argument.

"I'm not sure if Sarah wants to return for the Season, Mother."

Sarah loved being out of London, and he knew she wouldn't like having to share a house with his mother and sister-in-law in town.

"I do not care what that woman wants. You will return with us and do your duty to your family. Your father would be horrified to think that you let Honoria and me go to London without you. Who will be there to look after us?"

Oliver bit the inside of his cheek. He didn't care who looked after them, but she was right. It was his duty, his obligation, to make sure his mother and Honoria were safe. He could not do that from here.

"I will discuss it with my wife."

"You will do your duty for the first time in your life," his mother fairly yelled. "You have been nothing but a disappointment since the day you were born, and I will not have you failing us now."

Oliver cringed and reached for the port. How could he argue with her? He *was* a disappointment to her, and to his late father and his late brother. He was a disappointment to Sarah, too. He'd always known that he wasn't up to the task of a dukedom.

⁓

OLIVER PACED IN HIS BEDCHAMBER. Should he go into his wife? *Could* he go into his wife? After their horrible talk two days before, when he'd all but told her she wasn't good enough to be his wife, he hadn't felt free to touch her, let alone make love to her. Since his mother had arrived, the only moments of happiness they'd had were in Sarah's bed, and now he felt barred from that too.

He sat down on his own bed with a thump and called himself ten types of a coward. He hadn't even told Sarah that he would be returning to London with his mother. After being degraded and derided for the entire evening, not an unusual event, he had finally acquiesced and agreed to return with them, just to stop her picking on him.

Climbing into his vast, cold and lonely bed, Oliver had the urge to weep. Ultimately defeated on every front, he was a failure to the title of duke and all the responsibilities that came with it. He was a failure to his wife. She was miserable and alone. And most of all, he was a failure as a man, who could not even bring himself to apologise and seek comfort in his wife's body, as he knew she would offer.

That was probably the worst part. He was aware that she would never deny him, but did she still want him? After everything he had done and said, could she care for him the same way she had before? Did she still love him as she had? Because although the words had never been said, Oliver had seen her hurt and pain written ten feet high in her expression when she'd looked at him.

THE NEXT MORNING, after a fitful night's sleep, Sarah awoke to her maid beside her bed with a tray of tea, buttered toast, and a note from Oliver.

Terrified of what this note would say, she sipped her tea without opening it, trying to keep her nausea at bay. Once she was satisfied that she would not be sick, Sarah picked up the expensive paper and unfolded it, her breath hitching in her throat.

My dear,

Once you have awoken, would you please meet me in my study?

I have something to discuss with you.

Oliver

Sarah's heart sank. Pressing a hand to cover her baby, she took a deep, steadying breath. Whatever he had to say, she would endure it. Perhaps he had decided to take her away from here? Or he wanted to discuss sharing her bed again? Although Sarah tried to be as positive as possible, optimism coming naturally to her, she could not stop herself from believing that something dreadful was afoot.

With those hideous women in the house, anything was possible.

Sarah deliberately dressed in another of her old walking dresses, feeling comfortable and like herself. She made her way to the duke's study, smiling her thanks to the butler as he opened the door for her.

"Good morning, my dear." Oliver's voice sounded hoarse.

"Good morning, Oliver. Did you sleep well?"

Oliver's eyebrows rose, but he didn't comment on her odd tone.

"I did, thank you. And you?"

"Not particularly," she answered honestly.

"Sarah, you're not happy at the moment, and I'm not sure what I can do to change that. On Friday, I will be escorting my mother and Honoria back to London for the rest of the Season."

A cool calm descended on Sarah, stilling her racing mind. She blinked slowly.

"Do you wish to stay here, or would you prefer to come with me to London?"

Sarah heard the softly pitched words and real terror struck at her heart. How could Oliver abandon her? And worse yet, how could she go with him? She knew that his townhouse was half the size of this house, and she would never be able to escape the two other women there.

Gathering her courage, Sarah informed him of her decision. "Neither. I would like to go to Scotland, if I may."

She had spent the time whilst she dressed quizzing her maid on the other landholdings owned by the duchy. There were options other than here and London.

"To the old castle?" he asked, his eyes widening in surprise.

"Yes. Do you think there will be enough servants if I take my two maids with me?" Sarah forced herself to keep her eyes locked with Oliver's, but inside she was screaming with rage.

How could he choose to return to London when I need him with me?

"I'm sure there would be," Oliver answered slowly, frowning in thought. "I will send a letter ahead of you, but I doubt they'll need to do more than air and prepare your rooms. All of the properties owned by the duchy are well-staffed and can be ready at a moment's notice."

Sarah nodded and bowed her head. Clearly, Oliver was more than happy to pack her off to a distant castle. Why was she surprised? All of her initial fears about their marriage were coming true. Oliver would not miss her presence, and yet her heart ached as though it were being slowly pulled apart at the seams. Tears slid down her cheeks before she could stop them and she tried to wipe them away, subtly.

"I'm truly sorry you have been so miserable, Sarah."

"Oh, Oliver..." Sarah opened her mouth, ready to tell him how much she would miss him, how much she loved him, how much she wanted her baby to bridge the chasm between them.

She was stopped by the look in his eyes. Sarah saw nothing but regret and loathing. She didn't know whether it was directed at himself or her, but she knew this wasn't the time for such declarations. Especially while she was feeling so fragile.

If she declared her love only to be rebuffed, she didn't think her heart could bear it. She would have to wait until she felt a little stronger.

Standing up with as much grace as she could gather, she said the only words she could. "I'll go and start packing."

Chapter Sixteen

Oliver travelled the eight miles to London on horseback. His mother said she was truly scandalised, but he preferred her ten-minute outburst of displeasure rather than having to listen to her obnoxious blabbering in the carriage for the whole trip.

They settled into the Lincoln townhouse. Oliver took the duke's bedroom, his mother the duchess's rooms. Oliver hated that his wife wasn't in the chamber adjoining his.

If someone saw his townhouse, they would assume nothing had changed in his life. While inside, Oliver saw the world with entirely new eyes.

~

AFTER A MONTH FROM HELL, Oliver gave in to his mother's blatant attempts at making him feel guilty about, as she put it, never coming out into society as his title demanded.

He attended a ball.

He stepped into the music-filled room and glanced around the richly dressed, assembled members of the London ton. Hopefully, he could dance once with Charlotte or his sister-in-law and then hide in the card room.

He spotted the effervescent Lady Charlotte and moved quickly into the safety of her company and joined the gentlemen standing in her circle.

"Lady Charlotte," he said, greeting her with his best courtly bow and a smile. He had few real joys nowadays, but seeing his true friends was one of them.

"John, Archie." He nodded to his best friends standing near her.

Charlotte curtsied, and the gentlemen inclined their heads with a smile.

"Oliver, I didn't realise you had come back to town." Charlotte held out her hand, and he bent over her fingers and touched his lips to her glove.

The gentlemen shook their heads in agreement, and Oliver clenched his teeth, forcing a smile to his lips. He hadn't been looking forward to this conversation with his friends.

"I've been back for a while." *A whole month, but who's counting?*

"Haven't seen you at the club," Archie admonished quietly, his elegant eyebrows rising in question.

Oliver lifted a shoulder in a half-shrug, glancing away for a moment.

"I've been busy with estate business and have been working with my fencing master quite a bit."

Every day actually. It was the only thing keeping his body in check. It stopped him from mounting his horse and galloping straight to Scotland. Damn his pride. He wanted his wife.

"Not to mention the fact that you are newly married," Charlotte teased with a cheeky grin and a sisterly nudge to his side. "Where is that beautiful wife of yours?" Charlotte turned her head, apparently looking for the blonde angel who belonged at his side.

Oliver steeled himself for what he had to tell Charlotte, and for the response he was sure to get.

"Sarah has gone to Scotland for the rest of the Season." He explained as nonchalantly as possible. He glanced away again, then returned his gaze to her frowning face.

"Pardon?" Charlotte leaned forward, as though she hadn't heard correctly.

"Sarah's in Scotland." His cheeks ached as he tried to maintain his smile and there was a heaviness on his chest that he couldn't seem to dislodge. He coughed.

"I'm sorry, Oliver, I must not have heard you correctly."

Oliver wasn't enjoying the play of emotions across Charlotte's face. They made him feel sick with guilt. She had never hidden her feelings well. It was the one thing she didn't seem able to do. He clenched his teeth together and tried once more.

"Sarah's in Scotland." He said it this time louder and with more feeling.

"What did you do?" Charlotte swung exasperated eyes heavenward and then fixed them back on his face.

"Charlotte, please." Oliver wasn't sure what else to say as he watched her boil dangerously close to exploding. Her face was turning red, and her eyes were practically spitting fire.

"What did you do?" Charlotte repeated the question, then lowered her voice when she noticed how many people turned to look at them. She removed the scowl from her face and plastered on a calm facade, although it was obvious the fire beneath was still burning.

"I came back to London without my wife." Oliver repeated the words he knew had to be said, but he was loath to say them. It still hurt that she had chosen Scotland over him.

"And you packed her off to a Scottish castle? Your new wife? Your *duchess*?"

"She wanted to go. She wasn't enjoying being at the estate and when I asked her whether she wanted to come back to London with me or stay there, she chose to travel to Scotland instead."

"That is impossible. You must have done something very wrong." Charlotte shook her head.

"I didn't do a thing. The servants and I welcomed her. It was only when my mother and sister-in-law arrived, that—"

"*No!*" Charlotte's voice lost the calmness and she glared at him.

Oliver groaned. This was too much, even for him. And he had plenty of practice managing difficult women.

"You let your mother and that *snake* of a sister-in-law visit, while you were on your honeymoon?"

"They didn't visit. They live there."

"Oh Sarah, you poor, poor thing," she murmured as if to herself, clasping her hands in front of her ample bosom.

"Charlotte, that is not fair. I didn't do anything—"

"*Exactly*. You didn't do anything to protect your beautiful, sweet, innocent wife from being set upon by the most scheming pair of women I have ever met."

Oliver had forgotten that Charlotte and Honoria had debuted in the same year. They were both duke's daughters and had moved in the same circles. It seemed that Charlotte's opinion of Honoria was similar to Sarah's.

"You stupid, ignorant..." As Charlotte blew air out her nostrils and started to wind herself up into a full-blown attack, help came from an unexpected corner.

"Lady Charlotte." Archie stepped in front of Oliver and bowed to her.

"May I have the pleasure of this dance?" The question was politely worded, but his stance and tone left little to decipher.

Charlotte shut her mouth and eyed Archie with disdain.

"Of course, my lord." Her eyes flashed daggers at Oliver even while Archie led her away.

"I wasn't quite expecting that response," Oliver muttered to John, the only one still standing near him.

"Charlotte is very fond of Sarah." John gave him a confused look. "You didn't allow your mother and sister-in-law to intrude upon your honeymoon, did you?"

"Not you, too." Oliver was ready to throw up his hands in defeat. If John wouldn't defend him, no one would.

"No, don't get me wrong. If Sarah wanted to go to Scotland, then that's fine. But why did your mother and Lady Sombury leave London in the middle of the Season to visit you?" John pointed out, his eyebrows rising in a question that Oliver had never thought to ask.

"They said they wanted to help, but, well, they didn't."

He didn't understand why his mother hadn't left Sarah and him alone. He knew that she didn't approve of Sarah as the new duchess, but he hadn't had the courage to ask his mother to back off, let alone to leave her home.

Her home... that just said it all.

OLIVER BURIED himself for another month. When he finally resurfaced, he started attending his club, often spending the afternoons riding or talking with John, Archie or Rupert.

At his club, he placed a fake smile on his face when explaining that his wife had taken to the country for the remainder of the Season. Most of the gentlemen shrugged or gave him an understanding wink or nod. They probably thought he had discarded her, yet nothing could be further from the truth.

The one thing he couldn't force himself to do was indulge in an affair. He could hardly keep his food down when he thought of laying with another woman.

How could he ever touch another woman with the hands that had loved Sarah?

He was aware that everyone expected it. Rupert had gently suggested he look at finding a discreet mistress. He had been inches away from planting his fist on his friend's jaw.

One more month of the Season and he could return to his wife. He would find Sarah and demand they never separate again. Assuming that was, that she'd have him back at all.

AFTER AN AFTERNOON at his club listening to Archie complain about a ball his mother was forcing him to attend, Oliver decided he would make the effort to attend. Comrades in arms, and all that.

Oliver had been enjoying himself amongst his peers and friends in the card room, when a nasty voice broke through the cigars and sherry.

"Look who's here, and without his pretty wife." The snide comment came from behind John's back, and Oliver looked up to see a large man step out from his friend's shadow.

"Millington." Oliver inclined his head and turned back to Archie.

Patrick Millington moved around their group and took the seat opposite Oliver.

"So, how's married life?" he asked with a leer.

"Good."

"And where is the pretty new duchess?" Millington looked around the room as though he would see her there.

Oliver gripped his cards tightly in his hands, his palms beginning to sweat. He hadn't seen Millington since the night he had tried to make Sarah dance with him again, and Oliver had punched him in the stomach.

"She's in Scotland for the remainder of the Season."

For the first time, Oliver was glad Sarah wasn't in London. She would be horrified if she had to deal with this man again.

"What a pity." Millington sighed dramatically.

Oliver saw the interested looks they were getting from the gentlemen in the room, but did his best to maintain the illusion that he was in control of his temper.

He smiled and picked up his sherry, swallowing the sweet liquid with a harsh gulp.

John answered for him. "It is a pity. My sister especially wishes the duchess had returned."

"She's not the only one." Millington leered again and slapped John on the back. This time, Oliver smelled the liquor on Millington's breath and tried to unclench his fingers.

"Millington." John's tone was a warning as he moved restlessly in his seat.

Everyone in the card room was now watching their group. Oliver's face flushed with heat at being the centre of attention. The expression on Millington's face was satisfied, triumphant, and Oliver didn't know why.

He was the one who had won her; he had married her, taken her virginity and enjoyed months in her bed. Why was Millington looking so smug?

"Why do you care? She's nothing to you." Oliver shot back. Propriety be damned.

Millington laughed, the sound rough and too loud.

"But I was so hoping that she could be." His lustful eyes told Oliver more than his words could about what he wanted from Sarah.

"That is uncalled for." John surged to his feet in time with Oliver. Millington slowly followed. "Speak plainly, Millington."

Standing now, the bastard was within arm's reach.

"Oh, I just hoped now that she was married, Sarah would indulge herself like so many other married ladies."

Oliver lunged forward and wrapped his hands around the other man's throat, remembering the way Sarah had looked that first night.

"Over my dead body." He squeezed tight.

"Oliver, stop." John tugged at him.

Oliver forced his aching hands to relax and released Millington's throat reluctantly. He glared at the disgusting man, who was a mottled red, and turned to leave.

He heard Millington wheeze and cough, then speak. "You can't protect her night and day, do you realise that? When she's in London next Season, I will make sure she grants me an audience."

Oliver froze. As a married woman, Sarah wasn't as protected as virgins were. She was allowed to walk alone, ride in carriages alone and meet gentlemen in his home alone. Oliver had a vision of Sarah's lovely body held prostrate under Millington's, fighting him to no avail.

Oliver turned and swung, putting all his anger and pain behind his fist and hit Millington squarely on the side of the head. Pain splintered through his hand, and he roared. Millington went down and didn't get back up.

The rest of the night was a blur. A doctor was called, Oliver was rushed home, and a report was made to the authorities. No one blamed Oliver and as a duke, he was beyond reproach.

Millington regained consciousness the next day, with no lasting effects. Oliver only hoped he had the chance to plant the bastard properly the next time he saw him.

Chapter Seventeen

Many miles away in Scotland, Graves, Lincoln's butler, was indulging in a habit he rarely allowed himself. Gossip. His wife, the housekeeper, was worried about their new duchess.

"I don't like it, Isaac, I just don't like it," Mrs. Graves told her husband in bed that night. "She's clearly pregnant and miserable."

"Do you think the duke knows?" Graves asked.

How could the new duke he had known as a young man turn out to be so heartless? Her Grace was the most beautiful woman he had ever seen. She was also kind to the servants, clearly well-bred, elegant and thoughtful.

She was also definitely not born to be a duchess. She had been found making her bed, baking a cake in the kitchen and dusting the bookshelves in the library. Her actions would usually have sent the maids into a mad rush to stop her and do a better job themselves.

However, they had been warned of her need to do odd jobs like the dusting, through a carefully worded letter from the duke. Therefore, they had let her do whatever she wanted. In response, the duchess had seemed content.

"I don't know. But it would be horrible if he did. That would mean he got her pregnant, shipped her here, and then ran back to London to go back to bedding his whores," Mrs. Graves answered, with a shake of her head.

Graves clucked his tongue disapprovingly at his wife's language.

Mrs. Graves gave him that look which told him she knew exactly what young men did, and promptly turned over to go to sleep.

IN ANOTHER PART of the ancient castle, Sarah sat awake with a book.

She found it very hard to sleep most nights. Her back hurt already, and she only had a small bump. She didn't know how she would cope when she was bigger. Sarah put her book of French poetry aside and blew out the candles next to her bed.

The fire in the grate cast a small amount of light in the room, and she lay down, pulling her gown up to her waist. She ran her hands over her belly. Lying on her back, her womb seemed to distend, and she could feel the protrusion of her developing babe. Sarah took so much pleasure from her growing child that she rarely thought of Oliver, only once an hour or so. The small flutter of movement deep in her belly made her heart lighten. Oliver had given this child to her in a moment of love and passion.

She still didn't know why Oliver had withdrawn from her, but she knew it had everything to do with his family. As her husband and as a man, Oliver had loved her. He had laughed with her, cared for her and brought her incredible pleasure in his bed.

But as a son and the new Duke of Lincoln, he seemed lost, angry, upset and frustrated. Somehow, their marriage had become that too. Over the past two months, Sarah had realised that she could have done more to hold their marriage together. She could have stayed by his side, talked to him, or stood up to his family more often, and she was resolved to do so when she went back to London after the babe was born.

She had decided to stay in Scotland and birth her babe in the ancient castle. She was happy here. The servants treated her with respect and warmth. They smiled at her and listened to her and didn't get upset when she did things that normal duchesses didn't do.

When Sarah had arrived in Scotland, she had spent her nights trying not to cry into her pillows and her days wandering aimlessly around the glorious castle. But after two months of good food, clean air and reflection, she was determined to get her husband back.

Sarah's mother had visited for two weeks the month before. Her mother had taken one look at her and known what was going on.

"Daughter, it appears that you need to weep, long and loudly," her mother had told her, running a loving hand down her cheek.

Sarah had said, "I shouldn't, Mother, it's not good for the baby."

"Oh, nonsense, I spent half my pregnancies in tears over nothing and all of you are beautiful children. Come here."

And thus, given permission to grieve, Sarah had cried and cried. So many tears fell that she felt severely dehydrated after she was done. Her mother had held her, rocked her, and had told her everything was going to be all right. To have faith in herself, her husband, and God.

The only thing that still bothered Sarah was the thought of Oliver going to another woman in London. It tormented her daily, but she clung to the memories of their passion, hoping he would not need to replace her. She was terribly afraid, as most husbands in his peerage would take a mistress. But then she would remember his promise to be faithful, lay her hand on her belly and try to be positive.

THE NEXT MONTH passed in a blur of alcohol-fuelled days and nights for the Duke of Lincoln. Oliver lost himself in the bottom of a port bottle, or several port bottles, to be precise.

He lay his head back against the head rest on his chair in his study and heard his butler announce a Mister Turner through a foggy brain.

Why was Archie here? He opened his eyes and groaned at the sight of his friend's gold embroidered waistcoat.

"Archie, I will go blind looking at a waistcoat like that."

"I think the alcohol will do more to your eyesight than my clothes ever could."

Oliver moaned. "Don't lecture me." He let his eyes close, and his head fell back against the head rest again.

"Join me at the Mossam ball tonight." Archie put as much command into his voice as Oliver had ever heard.

He grunted in reply. His sister-in-law had more bite in her than that.

"We have allowed you a month to get over that incident with Millington. It is time you attended another event."

Oliver groaned again at the use of the royal "we." He could only imagine that Rupert, John, and Archie had been discussing him.

"Would you sit down, for God's sake?" Oliver gestured with his hands, annoyed that his perfect friend would be here to witness him in such a state. Why could they all not just leave him alone to be miserable?

Archie chuckled. Oliver opened his eyes at the sound. It had been a long time since Archie had laughed like that.

Seeming to remember himself, Archie schooled his face into impassiveness.

"Let's get you some coffee and then get you into your evening clothes."

Oliver allowed Archie to order coffee and something to eat. An hour later, he was feeling better and made his way upstairs for a bath and to prepare for his first ball in months.

Two hours later, he wished he had never let his friend drag him out of the house. Two widows had propositioned him, as well as a bored married matron. He could not wait to leave. Why did they not understand that he didn't want anyone other than his angel, Sarah?

Oliver could finally admit it to himself and would out loud if necessary. He missed Sarah. He loved her and no one else came even close.

He was walking past a small alcove off the side of the ballroom, when he heard his name being spoken. Oliver would usually have ignored it, but something in the tone arrested his attention.

He sidled closer but kept out of sight so that the women could not see him.

"I cannot believe you and your mother-in-law managed to run off the new duchess so quickly. I thought it would take you months."

A snide little laugh that he recognised very well rang in response.

"It was very easy, really. We hardly did a thing."

Yes, Oliver thought bitterly. Other than everything you knew to make Sarah feel about as welcome as a flea.

And I did nothing to help her. Self-disgust bloomed in his chest.

"No, really, tell me. I thought the greatest love match of the year would prove almost unbreakable."

Oliver swallowed the lump that rose in his throat. Was that really how the ton saw his marriage? If only it had been true. He'd thought they could get through anything, but at the first hurdle they'd both fallen. Or rather, he had and he'd taken Sarah down with him.

Another horrible laugh sounded.

"Hardly. All we did was let her fall on her pretty face. She didn't know how to organise an informal dinner at home. She couldn't instruct servants, and she dressed like a peasant. She found out very quickly that she wasn't suitable to step into *my* shoes." Honoria's disdain was so obvious now that Oliver could not believe he had ever thought the woman would help Sarah.

Fool.

"But what will you do now?" asked her companion, apparently eager for the gossip.

"Now? Nothing. Oliver is exactly where his mother and I want him. By our side in London, a country separating him and his wife. He is so malleable. Nothing like my dear husband, the real duke."

Oliver's backbone stiffened at this evidence of how his sister-in-law really saw him. He could only imagine how miserable she would have made his life if he had married her. Being compared to his brother for every day of his life? The thought was enough to weaken his knees.

"Malleable, how?" asked her eager friend.

"Well, just last week his wife wrote to him asking him to visit her in Scotland. During the Season, can you imagine that? Intolerable." Honoria sounded disgusted at the prospect, despite the fact that she had left London for a month to join him and his new wife at their estate.

Oliver tried to recall the day Honoria was talking about, but could barely remember. His butler had read him a letter whilst he had been in his cups.

"And he chose not to go?" the other woman asked, apparently surprised.

"Of course, he wanted to go. But his mother made it clear that his wife was just having a fit of the vapours and that she could wait another few months."

Oliver gasped and then quickly covered his mouth. He did remember his mother raving about something that night, but he rarely listened to her anymore.

"Oh, that poor woman." The stranger sighed.

"I know, it is rather amusing, is not it?" The glee in Honoria's voice was sickening.

"What newlywed bride wants to know that her new husband would prefer to be gallivanting around London than spend time with her? It must have broken her heart."

The sadness in the stranger's voice hit Oliver the hardest.

Was that really how Sarah would have seen his staying in London rather than following her to Scotland? He would never have let her go if he thought she believed he was carousing.

Honoria's laugh was genuine now. She was truly amused.

"Serves her right, if it did. She had no right to marry so far above her station." Honoria's voice was so full of the victory, she sounded ecstatic.

"But what is it she wanted, do you think?" the stranger asked.

Oliver began to move away from the column, sick with guilt. His belly felt tight, as though someone had gut-punched him.

"To tell him she is *enceinte*, probably," Honoria replied bitterly.

"*Enceinte*? Already?"

"Probably. The lower classes never seem to have any trouble."

Pain, unlike anything Oliver had ever felt, smacked him in the chest. He doubled over, breathing hard. Honoria was poisonous. He'd honestly had no idea how deep her treachery lay.

"Do you really think she could be carrying his heir, though?"

Oliver was wondering that himself. Thinking back, he had spent every night for almost eight weeks in Sarah's bed without her flux. The reality of that hit him like a slap in the face. Why hadn't he counted the weeks? Was she really pregnant?

"My maid told me of her suspicions even before she left for Scotland. They had all noticed her lack of monthly linens."

Pardon me?

Oliver huffed, breathing hard from his nose. His hands clenched into fists as his throat ached with the need to scream.

Honoria had thought that his wife was pregnant. And yet, she had not only encouraged Sarah's departure to Scotland but had intentionally kept him in London so that he would continue to be unaware of her condition.

"That won't make it easy to separate them, if that is what you intend."

"Well, you never know. If Oliver stays on past the end of the Season, she may have died in her childbed before he can even reach Scotland."

Oliver hadn't been aware of making any sound. But from the way the two women in front of him gasped and jumped, he realised he must have.

Sarah had been right all along. This woman was worse than horrible. She was evil. Why hadn't he just paid her to leave?

He may not feel like the Duke of Lincoln, nor did he want the title or feel as though he deserved it, but he was.

Dammit, he was. With all the power and money that came with it.

And it was finally time he stood up and took control of his own life and destiny.

"You, my lady, will never enter one of my homes ever again," Oliver growled at his sister-in-law as he rounded the pillar, his shoulders flexing and straining as his arms shook with anger. "My brother may not have allowed a large enough annuity for you, but I will. You will live wherever you want, marry whomsoever you want, but you will not come near me, my estate, nor my wife ever again."

"Oliver..." Honoria began.

Oliver straightened to his full height and glared down on her.

"My name is Lord Oliver Lyre, Duke of Lincoln. You will address me as such."

"Your Grace," she squeaked.

Oliver turned and left without bowing, without even a word of farewell. He grabbed his coat, hailed his carriage and headed home as fast as his team of six could carry him.

Chapter Eighteen

Oliver sent a note ahead to his Scottish estate, informing the servants that he would be joining his wife, but requesting them not to tell her, as it was a surprise.

He rounded the final bend in the road and looked out at the estate he had not visited in almost a decade. It was beautiful. Grand and ancient. He had always loved coming here as a child.

He was greeted by a young footman and the older, balding butler.

"Your Grace, it is splendid to see you here."

The old butler bowed and smiled.

Oliver searched his memory and came up with a name.

"Thank you, Graves, it's lovely to be here. Could you tell me where my wife is?"

The two footmen behind the butler shared worried looks and Oliver's stomach tightened with concern. Was she all right?

"Her Grace is walking the rose garden, Your Grace." Graves's eyes lit up at the use of Sarah's title.

Oliver could only assume his wife had found her place amongst his servants. Without the interference of Honoria or his mother, she was sure to have charmed them all.

Oliver followed a footman out to the gardens and stopped when he saw her. She was very clearly pregnant. Why she hadn't told him, he didn't understand, but it was clear that the condition agreed with her.

She glowed with good health. Her breasts had almost doubled in size and Oliver felt the stirrings of arousal for the first time in several months.

Sarah stopped along the path, bending backwards over her hand pressed into her lower back and looked toward the house.

She caught sight of Oliver and stared at him, blinking rapidly as though she expected him to disappear.

His heart pounded in his chest, and he inhaled slowly, forcing his heavy legs to walk over to his wife. He stopped and bowed to her.

"Sarah." His throat was tight with an unfamiliar emotion as she continued to stare at him.

Sarah gasped, "You're real."

Oliver laughed for the first time in months. "Of course, I'm real."

"But you wrote and said you couldn't leave London at the moment and wouldn't be coming to see me." The hurt he had caused her was evident now that he could see the black marks beneath her eyes.

"I know. Do you think we could go somewhere to talk?" he asked, conscious of the many servants now discreetly congregating around their duchess.

"Of course. My afternoon sitting room would be perfect."

She lifted her head and accepted his offered arm.

Oliver had spent the journey to Scotland rehearsing what he would say to his beautiful wife once he arrived. He knew he owed her many apologies, but where to start was the hardest question to answer. He had always found that being honest with Sarah worked best, but that would mean he would have to tell her everything. And the thought of exposing himself so totally was terrifying.

Sarah squeezed his arm as they entered her sitting room and let go of him. "I'm glad you decided to come, Oliver."

"I wasn't sure you'd want to speak to me after the way I treated you."

Her gazed dropped. "It wasn't you that treated me unfairly."

He waited, sure there was more to come.

She lifted her gaze and looked straight at him. "Why did you not protect me against them, Oliver?"

He swallowed hard. "I am so sorry, Sarah. I should have been your champion throughout the whole time my mother stayed with us, and I wasn't. I left you to defend yourself against the wolves, and that was terrible of me. I can only hope that you will forgive me."

Tears trembled on her lashes and she blinked them away.

"I forgive you, of course I forgive you Oliver. It just makes me so incredibly sad to think that you would let anyone treat me that way."

He grabbed for her hands.

"I promise you, Sarah, that I will never let anyone speak to you that way again. Nor will I dismiss your complaints and feelings as I did, which I know was my greatest mistake. How can I make it up to you?"

He'd do anything. Even live out here in Scotland if she wanted to. As long as he had Sarah, he was home. He could manage his family's estate through letters and short trips to London.

She squeezed his hands.

"I want you to work with me through our marriage. I don't want to ever feel so alone again."

He laughed. "Done. I will change your bedroom into a sitting room, or anything you want, and give away your bed to the poor. My Duchess of Lincoln will sleep in the duke's bedroom every night."

"Perhaps we could change my bedroom into a nursery instead," Sarah whispered.

Oliver cleared his throat.

"When you wrote to ask me to come to you here, was there something, in particular, you needed me for?" He smiled as she blushed and dropped her head.

"I did want to tell you something important, yes," she admitted softly.

Oliver's eyes lowered to her belly that was now barely visible beneath the material of her dress. "And that would be?"

Sarah looked up, and her eyes narrowed. "You really can't tell?"

Oliver laughed, stopped, then laughed again. "Oh God, it feels good to laugh again."

His cheeks ached from smiling, and his belly hurt in a strange way, too. He hadn't been happy in three months.

Oliver fought the urge to whisk her off to a bedroom and strip her clothes away. How desperate he was to get his hands on her again. But that would have to wait. They had things to discuss.

"I think I can see what you wanted to tell me, Sarah, but I believe it would be best if you said it instead."

Sarah smiled, her whole face lighting up as she seemed to realise his intention.

"I am bearing your child, my lord."

And there they were. The sweetest words he had ever heard.

Sarah stood up and moved toward him. Oliver stood as she reached for his hand and pulled it to her.

Oliver swallowed uncomfortably but allowed her to bring his hand to her belly. That first touch of his hand on the hard bump that concealed and protected his child brought a lump to Oliver's throat.

He brought his other hand up as well and held his child with both hands. The baby moved in response, and Oliver felt the tell-tale shift of flesh. Startled, he dropped both hands away.

Sarah laughed, pulling his hands back to her. "He's just happy you're here, Oliver."

"He?" Oliver drew Sarah onto the chaise lounge so they could sit together.

"I've decided it is a boy." Sarah shrugged and set her chin. She was obviously brooking no argument. He didn't mind, either way.

"All right. I have missed you so much." He brushed the hairs at the nape of her neck with his fingers and inhaled sharply as pleasure coiled deep in his gut.

$\sim$

"I have missed you too."

Sarah moaned as his hot, soft lips captured her mouth in a kiss so sweet and gentle that it brought tears to her eyes.

"Let me show you my bedroom," she told her husband. Confident in his need for her, she decided it was the time that she showed him how much she wanted him. How much she needed him.

"We should talk first, about... everything."

"No, later," Sarah urged, tugging Oliver faster down the hall. There would be days, months, years, to talk about all the ways they needed to strengthen their marriage.

But for now, she needed to feel that incredible closeness that she had only shared with this one beautiful man that she loved.

The butler and several footmen stood near the entrance to the stairs. Oliver opened his mouth to dismiss them, but Sarah knew it was her time.

"Thank you so much, Graves. My husband and I will be dining in our room tonight. Can you send dinner up at seven?"

She lifted her skirts and began to ascend the stairs, her husband hot on her heels.

Her heart was beating heavily in her chest. She could not believe she had just invited her husband to bed her in the middle of the day. But it had to be done. She could not think straight.

All the tension of the past three months seemed to be focused on driving her insane with desire. She could feel the wetness between her thighs. Her nipples peaked beneath her dress and she could barely wait for Oliver to close the door behind him. What had pregnancy done to her?

"Sarah, I'm not sure if we should do this before we've had a proper talk." Despite what he was saying he was tugging at his cravat and unbuttoning his waistcoat.

Thank goodness for that!

Sarah tugged at her gown, loosely-laced in front to allow for her expanding tummy.

"I only want to know one thing, my lord, before you touch me."

If he lied about this, she was certain she would know.

Oliver's hands stilled on his shirt buttons as he awaited her question.

"Anything, Sarah."

"Have you touched another woman since we have been apart?" She didn't drop her eyes for a moment, watching Oliver for signs of discomfort.

He seemed to relax visibly, his shoulders dropping as a soft smile graced his now calm features.

"Oh, Sarah, I haven't touched another woman since that first night I met you," he confessed, his honesty evident in his eyes.

Sarah could have sobbed with relief, but instead, she pulled the gown off her body and dropped it to the floor, standing in only her chemise before her husband. Her nipples tightened further as they pressed against the silk, and the warmth of the room kept her from shivering.

He took the few steps that separated them, pulling her body against him.

She reached up for him as he swooped down for a kiss so hungry it sent the already built fire in Sarah roaring to life.

Sarah pulled back and dropped down to her knees, the carpet soft against her skin.

She had spent the last month imagining what she would do to Oliver if she ever got him to herself again. She had planned a seduction based around his pleasure. She would make sure that he never left her again.

Her own body ached in anticipation of what was to come, but she'd happily wait for her own fulfilment if it meant giving him this.

"No, Sarah, you can't." Oliver gasped and pushed against her shoulder, trying to step back from her grasp.

Sarah smiled up at him, and with her eyes coaxed him closer again.

"I can. I want to. Please, Oliver." She was all but begging now, gesturing with her hands for him to come back to her.

"But you're my wife, and you're pregnant!" Oliver recoiled again with wide eyes and flailing hands.

Sarah laughed softly. "Exactly. My body hungers for you, Oliver. And I am your wife. I should be the only one to give you pleasure."

Oliver moved back within her grasp, looking encouraged by her words.

Sarah grabbed hold of his thighs and pulled him closer. She stared at his beautifully erect penis and was amazed again that this was what had given her a child. Smiling up at Oliver, she wrapped one hand around the base and pulled him closer with a hand around his thighs.

She stared down at the beautiful piece of flesh again and laughed as she watched it quiver with anticipation. At her laugh, a similar shiver swept through Oliver's whole body, and he groaned.

She ducked her head and sucked the beautiful, hot flesh into her mouth. It was hard but also soft, and slightly salty. She used her hands and moved up and down on him in a similar fashion that he had taught her to ride him.

He tried to pull away, but she held him tight to her. She wanted this.

"Sarah, stop, please, I'm going to…" Oliver groaned as she squeezed the base of him and moved faster. He threaded his hands into her hair and cried out as though his soul was being ripped from his body.

He jerked, spilling himself in spasms into her mouth. Sarah swallowed quickly and licked the tip once more. Oliver's knees began to shake, and she let him slip from her mouth.

Oliver tugged Sarah to her feet, and together they staggered the few feet to the bed and collapsed on top of the covers. He kissed her mouth and buried his face into her hair, seemingly embarrassed. She held him to her and heard him as he whispered into her ear.

"Thank you."

Sarah giggled, happiness filling her belly and making her feel a little lightheaded.

"You shouldn't have done that for me, though, it's not right." Oliver continued to speak to her, still hiding in her hair.

Sarah pulled back and made him look her in the eyes.

"So, you believe only whores can give their men pleasure like that?"

Her husband's eyes widened, and her cheeks heated as she used a word that she'd only said aloud once.

"I wouldn't know, my love. I've never had that done to me before. I just didn't think ladies did that sort of thing."

She grinned up at him, the weight of her anger lifting now that she knew how special she was to him. She wanted to be the one to bring him unknown pleasure.

"Oh, Oliver, you forget, I'm not just a lady, I'm your wife. My mother told me that everything you do to me I can do to you, and you had brought me pleasure that way before. So, I reasoned that it was possible to do it for you too."

Sarah laughed again and kissed his shoulder, tasting the sweet flavour of his skin against her tongue.

Chapter Nineteen

Oliver stared at his wife for a long moment. Was that really what her mother had told her? No wonder she had always been so eager and happy to do anything for him or let him do anything he wanted to her.

Remembering all the times he had brought her to climax with his mouth, he felt his already satisfied cock stir to life again. Sliding down the bed, he slowly pulled her chemise up over her burgeoning belly, exposing luscious breasts and golden curls.

"Perhaps I should return the favour, then." He smiled up at her, dipping his head to her nipples.

Sarah cried out when he licked first one hard, darkened nipple, then the other. She cried out again when he pulled one into his mouth and suckled greedily. She threaded her hands into his hair and held him there, urging him to suck harder.

Oliver continued to lick and sip at her nipples while he slid his hand between her silky thighs. She was so wet, he groaned. Unable to resist, he slid two long fingers into her, enjoying both her moan and the way her body bowed up in appreciation. He slid his fingers out and spread the moisture across that hidden bud and listened to her moan again.

Smiling to himself, Oliver pressed kisses to her belly, lingering over the stretched skin before moving down to paradise.

It didn't take long. Oliver flicked his tongue over her twice, inserted his fingers once more, and she shattered.

He didn't let her come down from her high but pushed at Sarah's shoulder so that she would roll over. She came up onto all fours so that she could roll how he wanted and accommodate their growing child.

Her beautiful, rounded arse came into view, and he knelt behind her to admire the curves of smooth skin. Oliver pushed gently down on her back and encouraged her to drop her head.

"Go down flat and open your legs for me," he whispered in her ear, the words arousing them both to even greater degrees.

Sarah parted her legs and put her elbows out for balance. Oliver saw her tilt her hips and watched the glistening slit come into view. The sight of her opening hit him right in the belly, and he gripped the warm flesh of her hips.

He inhaled slowly to calm himself, lined his cock up and buried himself to the hilt in one controlled thrust. Hot, wet flesh enclosed his entire shaft and a groan rumbled in his chest. She was tighter than he remembered and he had to clench his teeth against the need to explode immediately. He stroked her back softly, stilling his movements to give her time to adjust.

"Please, Oliver," Sarah moaned, moving her hips in the rhythm she wanted him to pursue.

"Have you missed me, Sarah?" Oliver asked her as he very slowly withdrew, the tip of his cock still embedded in her heat.

"You know I have."

"Have you missed me inside you, like this?" Oliver penetrated her as slowly and as deeply as he could. He gripped her hips tightly, stilling her gyrations.

"Please, Oliver."

"Please, what, Sarah? What do you need?"

He knew he was possessive and a little cruel, but since he had accepted who he was, he could not help letting these new and foreign emotions run free.

"You, please," she begged again, moaning as he penetrated deep, feeling her arse against his belly.

"Tell me." Oliver gripped her hips tighter.

"Harder, please. Deeper, more." Sarah moaned, rolling her hips and bucking against him.

Oliver's control snapped. She was wet and wanting him. He couldn't hold back any longer. He thrust ruthlessly into her, setting up a deep, pounding rhythm that reached her womb.

"You'll never leave me again." He rode her harder and faster.

"No, I won't." Sarah cried out, pushing her body flatter and raising her hips higher for him.

"You're mine, Sarah, do you understand? My wife, my love, mine."

Oliver couldn't believe the words that were leaving his mouth but knew he needed to say them, and she needed to hear them.

"Yes!" Sarah screamed as she flew apart and convulsed around him over and over again, coming harder and longer than she ever had before.

Oliver tried to resist, but her body milking his was just too erotic. A wave of pleasure hit him like a fist to the gut. Ecstasy overwhelmed him as he pumped his seed into her with a hoarse cry of pleasure.

His release seemed to trigger another smaller climax inside of her, and she cried out again and shuddered beneath him. They dropped forward and to the side to protect the babe, and fell into a deep and restful sleep.

Several hours later, Oliver awoke to a knock at the door that signalled their dinner had arrived. Not bothering to get up, he just looked down at his wife and sighed as happiness washed over him like a cleansing rain. She was back where she belonged, in his arms. And he was back where he belonged, by her side.

"My babe," Oliver whispered, gliding his hand over the hard, round belly in front of him. Sarah was still asleep, but Oliver could not rest a moment longer; he wanted her again.

He had assumed that a pregnant wife would dampen one's ardour. But soon after seeing Sarah, he realised that whether she was her usual svelte self or as big as a house, he would want her 'til the day he died. She was the most beautiful, sensual woman he had ever known.

Oliver didn't even wake her, he just rolled Sarah onto her side and stroked between her legs. Her folds were still slick, so Oliver moved his hand up until he could flick the extra sensitive nub. He fondled her for a moment or two, and when she, still half asleep, tilted her hips back invitingly, he lifted her leg up and forward, and slid into her from behind.

Oliver grunted his approval when Sarah came awake with a moan and tilted her pelvis to give him better access. He wrapped a hand around her breast, tweaking the sensitive nipple.

"I love you, Sarah." Oliver moved slowly into her scalding body, enjoying her depths, and then pulled almost completely out of her.

Sarah gasped and shuddered.

He had to tell her how he felt. "I love you for who you are, but I also love you for the person you make me want to be." Oliver moaned deep in his throat as she gripped him tightly inside her sheath. He shifted his hip angle and began pumping into her faster.

"Come for me, please, I need you." He was so hoarse he sounded ill.

Sarah shook her head and turned to look at him.

"I love you, please." He began moving slower so that she felt every inch as it slid inside of her. He moved the hand that was gripping her hip around to the flesh just above where they joined, and Sarah cried out in pleasure.

Sarah began moving her hips in time with his, and she closed her eyes.

Oliver felt her sheath tightening, and he hissed, "Yes," ruthlessly holding back his orgasm.

Just when Oliver's vision started to blur, he felt the change in her. Sarah cried out, and her body convulsed, Oliver held tight to her hips and with one more thrust, joined her.

SARAH LAY in the circle of Oliver's arms, completely happy for the first time in months. This was even better than it had been at the beginning of their marriage. He loved her now, and she finally felt secure in that knowledge.

"I love you, too." She looked up into the almost black eyes she knew better than her own.

"Never leave me again. I almost didn't survive it this time," Oliver said, kissing her quickly on the mouth, the move possessive and hard.

"I had to leave, Oliver. Your mother made me feel like the worst wife in the history of bad wives, and I couldn't keep pretending that I didn't miss you as you were, before they arrived."

Oliver pulled her tighter against his body, the heat and strength of him reassuring.

"You stopped coming to my bed," she whispered, the pain still very palpable.

"I know, I'm sorry. I drank too much port one night when my mother was being particularly nasty and could not make it to your bed. And then the next night I could not bring myself to do it either. I felt like I was failing you as a husband and failing my servants and tenants as the new duke—failing everyone, in fact—and I just could not, Sarah. Please, forgive me."

"I knew you were struggling with your new responsibility. I'm sorry I wasn't more sympathetic."

"You were. I just could not see past my own inadequacies. You did everything you could under the circumstances, more than any other lady would have."

"I knew I wasn't good enough to be a duchess, but I thought I could keep you happy in bed, at least." Salty tears stung her eyes. She didn't want to cry again, but she knew that they needed to talk about this and lay it to rest, once and for all.

"Sarah, I love you. I have loved you since you tried to comfort me at the opera only a week after we met. You make me feel like the most important person in the world, and after a lifetime of feeling superfluous, you are exactly what I need."

Sarah could hardly believe her husband meant those words, but as she looked into Oliver's eyes and saw that he was genuine, her heart began to sing.

"I need you to know something. You are more than I deserve. You are the best woman I could have chosen to be my duchess," Oliver told her confidently, earnestly.

"Then why did you let me believe that you agreed with your mother?" Sarah asked.

"The problem was that I believed I wasn't good enough to be the duke. I have been told since birth that I wasn't, and I always believed it. But I have finally realised that I am the duke, no matter what my mother says, and from now on I intend to act accordingly."

"How?" Sarah looked up at her beautiful duke. Proud, yet insecure and so beloved.

"Well, to start with, I need to start taking a more active interest in estate business. Talk to Archie about investments. Talk to my steward about the tenants. I also contacted the old Duke of Turret, a friend of my father who lives not far from here. We spent time at his estate when I was a child, and I always liked him. He and his wife never had any children. He would offer a wealth of knowledge I could learn from, and I think he would be an excellent mentor."

Oliver started listing off all the ways he could improve his holdings and the lives of his tenants, anxiously shifting his eyes to her face.

Sarah nodded encouragingly as Oliver began to smile.

"I know that you have never liked my sister-in-law, and given some of the things I heard her saying in London, I have informed her she is not welcome back in any of our homes. Ever again." Oliver's face took on a hardness that Sarah could not quite decipher, but his tone seemed furious.

"Really?" Sarah asked, amazed. She didn't like the woman, it was true, she almost hated her, but...

"Will she have to go back to living with her mother?" Sarah asked, biting her lip in concern.

"I have organised an annuity to be paid to her on top of what my brother left her, so that she can live wherever she wants. Just not with us."

Sarah frowned for a moment and then smiled cheekily.

"Like paying your mistress, you mean?"

Oliver sat up in bed, and her noble and beautiful duke stared down at her with a look of such horror that she burst out laughing, holding her belly as it rippled. It felt so good just to laugh.

Eventually she stopped, wiping the tears from her eyes.

"I'm sorry, Oliver, but your face..." She broke off into another round of giggles.

"I'm glad you aren't angry that we will be paying for her upkeep."

"Of course, I'm not, Oliver. She is your brother's widow. The estate should keep her, just not in our home. I wish you'd thought of it sooner," she teased with a knowing look.

"I wish I had, too. It would have saved us a lot of heartache and I would not have missed these months with you. And hurt you so much." Oliver looked down at her with sad brown eyes and swept his hand lovingly over her belly.

"I CAN'T BELIEVE you got with child so quickly."

Sarah blushed. She wasn't sure if that was a good thing or not. She still wasn't sure if Oliver was happy about the baby or just glad that his heir was already organised.

"You're content with that, Oliver? I hope you're as happy as I am about the baby," she asked, trying not to sound as anxious as she felt.

Oliver sat up and leaned forward, pressed a kiss to her swollen belly and murmured, "I love you," against her skin.

Tears pricked Sarah's eyes, and she wiped them away before he could see.

"Now, tell me what you have been doing these past months. No more distracting me." Sarah flapped her hands at him, forcing him back up to eye level. "Please, Oliver," she all but begged, pressing a hand to his face, cupping his jaw in a loving way.

He sighed.

"I spent the first month fencing with my instructor and ignoring everyone. The second month was going to my clubs and the third month, drinking myself into oblivion every day."

Oliver exhaled sharply, his pain a tangible thing.

Sarah gasped. "I imagined you enjoying London's pleasures."

"I could not find pleasure in anything away from you." Oliver leaned forward to kiss her lips when they parted in surprise.

"Then why did you seem so relieved when I said I wanted to come to Scotland?" Sarah asked, determined to get all of her questions out of the way so that they needn't bring this subject up again.

"Because I knew you were miserable." His eyes welled up as he said the words and she rushed to reassure him.

"I was miserable, but never because of you. I blame myself..." Sarah started, silencing him when he was going to interrupt by pressing a hand to his soft lips. "I shouldn't have let your family upset me so much. I should have talked to you more. I let them come between us," Sarah said sadly, bowing her head in acknowledgment of her guilt.

"It was my fault, Sarah. I know it was. They hurt you because they knew it was the best way to hurt me. And I let it happen."

Sarah sighed heavily and leant across the bed to give her husband a soft kiss on the lips. She lingered and coaxed him with her lips until he rolled half onto her.

"Let's decide never again to let anyone else come between us. We'll always talk to each other first," Sarah suggested, pulling back to look into his eyes.

He nodded and swooped down for a kiss that turned into a loving and a worshiping of each other that lasted far into the night.

Epilogue

Three months later

Oliver paced the hallway, his shoulders aching and his arms stiff from the stress.

Another inhuman groan sounded from the door to his right, and he twisted around to pace down the hall runner once again.

"You really should stop that, Oliver. You'll wear out the rug, and your shoes." Archie's voice made him jump.

"I almost forgot you were here."

Archie lifted his head and gave him an incredulous look over the pages of his book. "Really?"

He gave his friend a smile, and Archie went back to his book. Archie had travelled up to see them a few weeks ago and had been excellent company for both he and Sarah.

The sun had risen while his wife had laboured all night. Her moans had turned to screams, and now they were grunting cries. He was tired and hungry, but nothing would move him from their bedroom door.

"It should be over soon, yes?" He shot an imploring look at Archie.

"How would I know?"

A loud bang sounded, and voices rose through the house, the cacophony of female voices and stomping feet getting closer and closer.

A loud wail broke through the sound, and his heart stopped for a moment.

A cry. A thin, small cry.

Oliver's heart began beating once again, filled with a bigger, brighter love for his wife than before. His child was here.

"Where is the woman?"

Oliver's heart sank. His mother was here!

The dowager duchess walked straight up to him, her nose high in the air.

The butler stood behind her with several footmen, all looking flushed and out of breath.

"It's fine, Graves. Please wait by the stairs. My mother will not stay long."

His mother's nostrils flared, her eyes sharpening like the lines in her face, making her seem hawk-like. Cruel.

"This is my home. I will stay as long as I like."

"You will not. You may say what you came to say, which is, of course, of great importance, or you would have put it in a letter."

A knock sounded, and the door to his bedroom opened. Oliver turned toward the midwife, her white apron smeared in blood.

"You have a son, Your Grace."

A tingle at the back of his throat signalled impending tears, so Oliver swallowed hard and walked forward, nodding at the midwife as he passed through into his bedroom.

It was hot, the moistness in the air and the heat from the blazing fire making perspiration bead on his upper lip.

Sarah sat in their bed wearing a white nightgown, her hair down around her shoulders as she lay propped up with pillows.

"Oliver. Look, isn't he the most beautiful thing in all the world?" Sarah's voice quivered as she stroked the still bloodied face of the baby in her arms. She looked pale and exhausted, her hair matted with perspiration.

"You are the most beautiful woman in the world." He sat upon the bed, stealing an arm around her and planting a kiss upon her head.

He hadn't been able to admit his fear, even to himself, but as the knowledge that they were both alive and well sunk in, relief washed over him like the waves of a storm. Cold, abrupt and with great relief.

"What should we call him?" he asked her.

The unwelcome voice came from the doorway. "Gerald, of course. After your grandfather."

Sarah froze, her shoulders becoming stiff beneath his arm.

His mother was inside his bedroom.

A place she was not welcome.

Oliver turned to her, cringing at the woman who stood at the base of their bed staring down at his son with a strange look of glee. She would be pleased he had an heir. Their line would continue. Her bloodline.

"You have no business here, Mother. Leave. Now."

She ignored him, walking around the bed to peer down at their son. "Where's the wet nurse? Call her this instant. Your wife is exhausted."

"I'm feeding him myself, Your Grace."

Sarah opened her white gown and exposed her creamy breast to their son, the squirming infant latching on quickly, contented sounds filling the air around them.

"Disgusting." His mother all but spat the word as she took a step back.

Sarah visibly cringed, and Oliver's control snapped.

"That is enough, Mother."

Oliver stood up and walked around the bed, grabbing the dowager by the arm.

"Remove your hands from my person this instant!"

She shrieked as he pulled her, bodily, from the room. His hands clenched her too tightly, but the anger in his belly grew worse as she screamed for help.

Hopefully, Sarah would forgive him for this.

He pulled her through the ante-room and out into the hallway and practically threw his other toward Graves.

"Graves, make sure my mother is packed off to London within the hour."

"You cannot do this, Oliver! I forbid it!"

"You forbid it! *You* forbid it? Mother, this is my home, not yours. I have told you that you may keep the London townhouse, but all the other property is now mine. You are forbidden from seeing my son, and my wife, and if you dare to intrude in our life once more, I will cut you off without a penny."

"You wouldn't dare."

Oliver took his time, glancing down his mother's expensive dress and up again, his gaze lingering on her jewelled necklace.

"Try me." His voice was deadly quiet and his mother cringed back. Yes, she had heard the truth in his words.

He stood straight, inclined his head and walked back into his bedroom, confident Graves would see to his wishes.

Back inside, the darkness enfolded him, relaxing Oliver once again.

"I am so sorry, my love. I promise that will never happen again."

Sarah glanced up at him, still feeding their son. "I heard what you said to her. You're sure that's the right thing to do?"

He bent down and placed another kiss on her head, smiling as she turned to get closer to him.

"Yes, my beautiful wife, it is. You, and our child, are the most important people in my life. Nothing will hurt you, ever again. For as long as I live."

Sarah nestled into his arms, and they sat there for many hours admiring every curve and wonder of their new son. Their world was only beginning, and Oliver would work as hard as he could, to make it a wonderful life, for all of them.

THE END

Download book 2 now:
https://books2read.com/u/br16Lw

Or read on for a sneak peek into the next story in 'The Heir and the Spare'
series.

Lady Charlotte's Ruined Marquess

Prologue

Ten years earlier

"Your father wishes to see you, Archibald," the Marchioness of Hunting announced to the quiet room in which they sat, her red-rimmed eyes puffy and fragile looking.

Archie's once-happy heart dropped so low he was surprised he couldn't see it lying on the carpet at his feet.

He dragged himself out of his chair and walked the few steps across the room to the heavy wooden door that marked the entrance to his father's domain.

His trepidation was almost crippling. His hands shook, and his desire to run away was so strong that Archie had to lock his knees in place so that he didn't do what his instincts were screaming at him to do. He hung his head for a moment, squeezed his eyes shut, then released a long breath.

It was time to face his destiny.

He lifted his head and stared at the mahogany wood, raising his still shaking hand and knocking on his father's study door.

"Enter." His father's hoarse voice sounded through the solid barrier and Archie squared his shoulders.

Archie turned the silver knob, pushed open the door and saw another set of red-rimmed eyes, matching his mother's.

Archie gasped and bowed low to his father to disguise his surprise. His father couldn't have been crying, surely? There had to be another reason for his appearance. Perhaps it was the result of heavy drinking and fatigue? Archie could only hope.

"Sit down, Archibald," his father commanded, his strong voice croaking and rough.

Archie almost tripped over the rug in his haste. His father had never before asked him to be seated in his presence. He had certainly never used his Christian name before in such a way. Archie could only hope that his father might be about to comment on his upcoming birthday, although his detached and logical brain knew that this thought didn't fit in with the visible tears which he had seen his cold, aloof mother and his proud, drunken father shed.

"Archibald, we have received some bad news and it seems that your brother will no longer be inheriting the Marquisate."

This life-altering statement was delivered with all the excitement of a eulogy. Archie's father had always been proud of his eldest son. It had been obvious in both his actions and words. Archie's older brother was the charismatic, arrogant and handsome heir who had always looked and acted just like their father.

He cleared his throat and tugged on his cuff. "Pardon, sir? Do you mean that Arthur will not be inheriting?"

"Do not speak back to me!"

Shock ricocheted through his system, yet he schooled his features into an expression of proper regard with practiced ease. He had spent the last five years as part of a group of four youths referred to as 'The Spares'. The four members were all the second sons of rich, old and powerful families. None of these friends wanted his father's title, nor the responsibility that came with it. Archie felt the same way. To be told that he would have to forget all his plans for the future, of managing his money and breeding horses, was devastating. He felt sick to his stomach.

"My apologies, sir." Archie bobbed his head in a seated half-bow, his head spinning with questions. What was he going to do now?

He sat still and waited for his father to continue. He needed more information, but with the unbalanced mood his father was in, Archie knew better than to push.

The older man appeared to be mulling the words over in his head, twirling his empty liquor glass around in his hands.

"Arthur is dying. He has indulged in his taste for loose women far too freely and now he is going to die."

His father shook his head sadly.

Archie was completely shocked. If he had been standing, he doubted he would still have been upright. Was his brother dying? He knew Arthur had not been feeling well recently, but dying? And from the dreaded French disease? Archie was not close to his older brother, as there were more than six years between them, but he didn't want him to die.

Whilst Archie was trying to digest this new information, his father hit him with the next verbal sledgehammer.

"So, you keep yourself clean. Understand me? Stay away from the whores and make sure you marry a woman who will be able to handle the scandal when it comes. We will be sending your brother to Italy for an extended holiday, but if word ever gets out, the family's reputation will be ruined."

Archie felt his heart stop. Was his father asking him to stay away from women? For how long? His friends had already organised his eighteenth birthday. A night of drinking and his first time in a brothel, his first female.

Did his father mean that he couldn't bed a woman until he married?

As Archie's mind raced with the implications of what his father told him, he felt his heart slowly disappear. It shrivelled up, just like a grape left on the vine too long.

His father was telling him that he was to inherit everything. The estate, the servants, the title, the responsibility. Everything, including a name that would forever be remembered for his brother's grotesque death. The society in which Archie wanted to be accepted would soon scorn him. What woman would want him? As Archie thought about all the lost possibilities, he realised that his life would never be the same again.

Chapter One

London 1812

Lord Archibald Turner, Archie to his friends, was the second son of the Marquess of Hunting. Archie had spent the last decade living an exemplary life. The epitome of gentlemanly behaviour, habits, and dress, without any of the excesses frowned upon but secretly tolerated.

He hardly drank, he didn't gamble, and he was a twenty-seven-year-old virgin. This, of course, meant he had never compromised anyone and had never taken advantage of the offers which were passed his way by the many unhappily married women in the *ton*. Archie spent more money on his clothes than all his friends combined, but that meant he always looked attractive and civilized.

Archie had spent the last six years fighting an intense attraction for one amazing woman. She was the only person who noticed him as more than the holy saint he pretended to be. She fought with him in public, teased him blatantly and laughed her full-bodied laugh at him. She was the only woman he had ever loved, and he wasn't sure how much longer he could bear standing close to her without declaring his intentions.

Lady Charlotte Dunford.

Archie groaned as his wayward member stiffened in response to said woman's laugh and the accompanying wobble of her generous breasts. He was wearing dark grey breeches that were so tight, they revealed everything. Archie had muscular thighs, unlike most of the men in the *ton* and his tailor often had trouble cutting his breeches just right. This wasn't usually a problem, but when the front of his breeches was quite visible due to a high-waisted white waistcoat and cut away evening jacket, Archie began to panic. Desperate for something that would douse his ardour, he thought back to the last time he had seen Charlotte.

It had been almost nine months before.

Archie had been standing with his friend of over fifteen years, the former Lord Oliver Lyre, now the Duke of Lincoln. Oliver had shown up to a *ton* ball, without his new wife. Oliver had been explaining why his wife was in Scotland, rather than by his side in London, when Charlotte had become incensed and started scolding him, in the middle of a crowded ballroom.

Lady Charlotte Dunford, his heart, his soul, the only woman Archie would ever want to marry. She was the only daughter of the Duke of Arrow, his friend Lord John Dunford's younger sister, and the most beautiful woman Archie had ever seen. She was also a woman with a keen mind and a nasty temper when aroused, and unfortunately, Oliver had excited it that night.

"You've done what?" Lady Charlotte raised her voice at the Duke, casting angry eyes heavenward and then fixing them back on to Oliver's face.

Archie wanted to put his hands over his ears to block the sound but gallantly squashed that ungentlemanly urge.

"Lady Charlotte, please," Oliver said.

Archie wasn't sure why Oliver, Duke of Lincoln, had let his duchess, Sarah, leave him to go to Scotland, but he felt perfectly sure that a public reprimand was not the way to go about finding out.

It was a pity that Lady Charlotte hadn't felt the same way.

"You've done what?" Lady Charlotte spat at him, quieter this time.

She removed the scowl from her face and plastered on her polite facade. Society did not approve of displays of excessive emotion and frowned upon public spectacles. Archie watched Lady Charlotte's attempt to conceal her feelings and could have told her not to bother. Lady Charlotte, having been a spoilt and indulged only daughter, had never been forced to school her features. She was, therefore, atrocious at pretending to feel calm when she felt otherwise.

"I returned to London without my wife." The duke repeated the words, obviously upset to be admitting the fact. His face flushed, his gaze darting around the room.

"And you packed her off to a Scottish castle? Your new wife? Your duchess?" Lady Charlotte enunciated each word calmly, her expression remote, but her words dripped venom. Archie held his breath. This was going to get horrid in a short time.

"She wanted to go. She wasn't enjoying being on the estate, and when I asked her whether she wanted to come back to London with me, or stay there, she chose to travel to Scotland instead."

Archie found this rather odd. He knew Oliver's wife, Sarah. He had seen the couple on their wedding day. Unlike most couples of the *ton*, who married for financial or social reasons, Oliver and Sarah's marriage had been a love match. Why had it gone wrong so quickly?

"What did you do?" Lady Charlotte asked again.

Archie could see the anger in Charlotte's eyes, he could feel the current of rage in her body, as though it was his own. He had always been able to do that. He could read her like no one else seemed able to do, not even her brother.

"I didn't do a thing. The servants welcomed her, and I took the utmost care to ensure her comfort. When my mother and sister-in-law arrived, they tried to—"

"No!" Lady Charlotte exploded.

Archie heard Oliver's groan and wished he could do the same thing. Must she always be so passionate about everything?

"You let your mother and that *snake* of a sister-in-law visit you while you were on your honeymoon?" Charlotte was incredulous.

"They didn't visit. They live there."

Charlotte seemed shocked by Oliver's reasoning, and Archie knew she didn't understand. She would never know what it was like to feel like you weren't wanted or needed by your parents. Once upon a time, he had felt the same way and it seemed that Oliver still did. Why else would he have allowed his relatives to invade what should have been his home?

"Oh Sarah, you poor, poor thing." Lady Charlotte murmured to herself, clasping her hands to her breasts.

"Lady Charlotte, that is not fair. I didn't do anything." Oliver protested again; Archie could have told him it was pointless.

"Exactly, you didn't do anything to protect your beautiful, sweet, innocent wife from being set upon by the most cunning, jealous pair of women I have ever met."

Archie raised an eyebrow, wondering which woman other than the dowager duchess that Lady Charlotte meant. Probably Lady Honoria, Oliver's sister-in-law.

"You stupid, ignorant—" As Lady Charlotte started to wind herself up into a full-blown attack, Archie gathered his courage and quickly stepped into the line of fire.

"Lady Charlotte," he interrupted, moving in front of Oliver and bowing to her. "May I have the honour of this dance?"

Lady Charlotte shut her mouth and eyed Archie with disdain. Archie made sure his body language left her no room for argument, and he stood in a way that completely blocked Oliver from her line of vision.

"Of course, my lord," she managed, her eyes flashing daggers around him at Oliver even while Archie led her away.

Her hand on his arm felt like a burning flame to his coat. He had avoided dancing with her since her coming out ball and this was the reason why. He had always hoped that his reaction to her would decrease; hoped his body would learn not to be so sensitive to her, but it had never happened.

She had as much effect on him today, as every other day since he'd met her.

Archie pulled Lady Charlotte gently into a waltz position—it had to be a waltz; bloody bad luck—and started moving her expertly around the room. Neither of them had spoken yet, but her eyes spoke volumes. Lady Charlotte had now divided her anger and Archie wasn't sure if he would fare worse or better than Oliver.

"Go on. I know you want to," Archie encouraged, schooling his face into his usual mask of politeness. He had thought that after a decade of pulling this face, it would be second nature and no longer feel false. But when he was with Charlotte, every feeling was intensified, to the point of being almost painful.

"I have nothing to say."

Archie bit back a smile. Lady Charlotte never addressed him, never had. He found it quite funny. He had no title, so she couldn't refer to him like that. He had never given her leave to call him Archie, and yet having been around her brother for most of her life, she could call him anything she wanted. And yet Lady Charlotte didn't. She avoided referring to him at all, and if she was pressed, she occasionally called him 'my lord', with a wry twist to her lips.

Charlotte's expressions were transparent; Archie could see every thought, every feeling as they crossed her face. At the moment, though, it didn't take a person familiar with Lady Charlotte to deduce her feelings. Her rage was there for the whole world to see. Her face flushed, her eyes narrowed and fired with passion.

"Lady Charlotte," Archie began. She hissed at him through her clenched teeth.

He had always addressed her as Lady Charlotte, partly because it was her title, due her because of her fortunate birth, but also partly because it annoyed her. For the first time since Archie had met Charlotte, he didn't ignore her glare.

"Well, what would you like me to call you?" he snapped, letting some of his annoyance slip into his voice. Her lips parted and her eyes widened, measurably. Archie didn't know if it was due to the tone of his voice or from his wording, but he couldn't take the words back now.

She opened her mouth to reply, then shut it again.

Archie waited. He danced them around the room, and he waited some more. Charlotte looked beautiful when she was angry. Her too-full lips parted slightly, and her bluer-than-blue eyes gave him a penetrating look, as if she was trying to read him. He knew she wouldn't see anything revealing on his face, but it never seemed to stop her from trying to understand him.

"Charlotte," she answered finally, her eyes wary as she awaited his response. "Well, Charlotte, say what you are thinking, so you can feel better."

Archie tightened his hold on her reflexively, as he feared she would leave him on the dance floor if she got angry with him.

"May I call you Archie?" She burst out with this question, instead of answering him.

He almost laughed out loud and smiled, despite himself. He had meant that she should vent her anger at him, not ask for his permission to use his name.

"Of course." He inclined his head. Her spine stiffened again, her hand going rigid in his grasp.

He groaned internally. Why was it that everything he did seemed to annoy her?

"Archie, how dare you pull me away just because I was angry with Oliver? He deserves to know what an imbecile he is. Doesn't he realise that Sarah will be heartbroken that he has abandoned her for his pursuits in London?"

Archie frowned. How could Charlotte know this?

"Firstly, I did not pull you away. I asked you to dance." He tightened his hold on her hand, as though to illustrate the point.

"For the first time in five years," Charlotte muttered under her breath, looking down and away from him. "And right at that moment."

Archie inhaled against the sudden pain in his chest. She sounded upset that he hadn't danced with her regularly over the years. If only she'd known the torment he felt every time another man held her, she wouldn't have been so quick to chastise him about the time they had spent apart.

Ignoring her jibe, he continued.

"Secondly, how can you be so sure of Sarah's feelings?"

Was this something ladies discussed? Or was Charlotte making assumptions?

"Because that was always Sarah's biggest fear about marrying above her station. The day before they married, she told me that she would never survive if Oliver chose another woman over her, if he took a mistress, or decided to gallivant around London instead of being with her. He is not only doing that, but he made sure she was in a different country, where she can only assume the worst."

In typical Charlotte fashion, she was not only discussing a topic that any unmarried lady of breeding would avoid, but she also spoke with such passion that Archie wished he could kiss her, suck on her lips until they bruised.

Archie closed his eyes as the longing coursing through him made him want to drop to his knees and beg her to be his. He slowed their dancing as the orchestra stopped, his palms beginning to sweat. One day, he would do something very foolish when it came to Charlotte. He could only hope it didn't occur in a ballroom full of people.

"Charlotte, if you like, I could speak to Oliver. I don't believe he is happy to be away from his wife."

Archie led Charlotte away from the dance floor, dropping her hand as quickly as he could.

"It doesn't matter whether he's happy or not. She must be miserable."

And with that declaration, she stormed off.

Archie suddenly came back to the present with a jolt and smiled at the memory he'd just been reliving. That had been the last time he had enjoyed a real conversation with Charlotte.

It was now nine months later, the beginning of another season, and she was miraculously still unattached. Archie watched her twirl around the room in the arms of a wealthy young lord and found himself wishing she would get married so he could also find someone suitable to marry. He could never commit himself to another until she was settled. It didn't make sense of course, but Archie couldn't bring himself to marry while Charlotte, the one and only woman he had ever really desired, was still available.

"Archie." Oliver approached with a genuine smile and shook his hand with vigour. Oliver was wearing a rose-coloured waistcoat, a black evening coat, and breeches. It sat very well on him.

Archie smiled warmly, his heart lifting at the sight of the Duke of Lincoln. His friend had never looked better, or happier.

"You look well, Oliver. How are things?" Archie asked although he already knew that everything was well.

"Excellent. Thanks to your advice, my finances have never been better, and my new estate manager has everything running smoothly."

Oliver had been the second son of the late Duke of Lincoln, and he had once confided to Archie that his father had told him that he would never inherit, so there was no reason to teach him anything about being a duke.

So, when at twenty-five years of age, Oliver had unexpectedly inherited the estate, he'd had no idea how to manage anything, let alone a dukedom. He had floundered considerably. Not only concerning the needs of his property and his many dependents such as servants and tenants, but also concerning his position in society, where he was expected to fulfil the role of a duke to the manner born.

"And your family?" Archie asked.

"Sarah's extremely well, thank you, and my son is wonderful."

The pleasure Oliver felt in being able to say those words was apparent. And when Sarah, his beautiful wife, glided up, her rose silk gown complementing her husband's attire, she slid her hand into the crook of his elbow. Oliver seemed to glow like the stars.

"Archie," Sarah greeted him warmly, her smile mirroring her husband's.

"Your Grace." Archie couldn't resist addressing the lady before him with her new title, bowing deeply over Sarah's outstretched hand and placing a chaste kiss on her knuckles.

Sarah blushed crimson, the colour extremely becoming on her. She had been born a clergyman's daughter, and Archie knew that she was still a little overwhelmed about the title she had inherited upon her marriage to Oliver.

She tapped at him playfully with her fan, reminding him that he should address her only by her first name. Archie laughed. His friend was very lucky.

❧

ACROSS THE ROOM, Lady Charlotte Dunford watched the scene between Archie and their mutual friends, the Duke and Duchess of Lincoln, with a warmth heating her face. She averted her eyes.

Why did Archie never tease her like that? Why did he never smile at her like he was smiling at the duchess right now? *Because he thinks you're a spoilt little girl*, the cynical voice in her head reminded her.

Archie had been friends with her brother, Lord John Dunford, since Charlotte had been a child. Five years younger than John, she had been barely eight years old when she'd first met Archie. She had thought him polite, but nothing more. At eight years of age, she wasn't interested in boys and her brother's solemn friend had not commanded her attention. When she had reached sixteen and had become a debutante, she had seen Archie as the man he was. Twenty-one years old, handsome as sin and as proud as a peacock.

He had danced with her once. As her brother's friend, he had been obliged to ease her way into society by offering to dance with her. Charlotte had felt safe with him, knowing he wasn't assessing her suitability as the perfect wife, as some of the more mature gentlemen had been. He had been polite but distant, and he had kept that distance for six years.

No, that was untrue. This dawned on Charlotte as she reflected on their association. They had also danced once, the previous year. Charlotte sighed at the memory.

She recalled how she had been furious at Oliver. Archie had whisked her away for a dance to prevent her from scolding his friend in public, thereby creating a spectacle. Archie was loyal to those he loved; he always had been. John always said that you could count on Archie to do the right thing, no matter the cost to himself.

During that waltz, Charlotte had finally seen a little of the real emotion Archie could express, which she had been looking for since she'd been a young girl. He had cracked open his mask for just a moment, and she had been surprised. Shocked senseless, in fact. Lord Archibald Turner was not a heartless machine, it seemed. He had feelings; she just wasn't sure how many, or exactly what they meant. Either way, he had captured her attention that night.

Now, raising her social armour and breezing effortlessly across the ballroom, she approached the young Duchess of Lincoln, feeling her traitor of a heart beating with a fast pace in her ears.

"Charlotte!" Sarah cried happily, her whole face lighting up with joy.

She looked so well, was Charlotte's first thought. Sarah had always been slightly pale and a little thin, but now she glowed with happiness and was nicely plump after giving birth to her son just three months previously. She was also wearing a rose silk gown that beautifully complemented her creamy skin and blonde hair, not to mention the newly acquired curve of her bosom, which only added to her beauty.

Charlotte leaned forward and gave the Duchess of Lincoln a quick hug.

"Sarah, I have missed you," she told her friend, honestly. She hadn't seen Sarah in almost a year, not since her wedding. Sarah had disappeared on her honeymoon and then hadn't returned to London.

Sarah's eyes glistened slightly and then she smiled brightly.

"I have missed you too, although I do remember a particular invitation from Scotland that you declined." She teased her friend, poking her lightly with her fan.

Charlotte suppressed a sigh. She would have loved to visit her friend in Scotland after her baby had been born, but the combination of envy for her happiness and respect for the young couple's need for privacy had kept Charlotte in London.

"I would have loved to visit you, my friend, but I knew how much you enjoy having your husband to yourself," she replied, giving Oliver a sharp glance.

The duke looked at the floor. He must have recalled that the last time he had seen Charlotte; she had railed at him for leaving Sarah alone in Scotland.

She smiled to herself, feeling so glad that she had.

"We all know that you never leave London, however odd that is, Lady Charlotte. Scotland would be far too uncivilized for you." Archie's cold voice broke into the conversation and Charlotte's gaze moved toward him. *How dare he try to make me look selfish in front of Sarah?*

"Lord Archibald, good evening, sir," she replied haughtily, giving Archie a half-curtsey.

He bowed low in return. He was a marquess' son, but he was the second son, and she was the daughter of a duke. As they were both unmarried, she outranked him.

"I rarely leave London, it is true, but I would have loved to have visited Sarah," she repeated, daring him to contradict her again.

Archie would usually have ignored any attempt of hers to bait him, yet tonight, she was succeeding while barely trying.

"How can you say that you would have loved to have ventured to Scotland when you rarely even visit Hampshire in the off season?" he asked with a raised eyebrow.

"That's only because—" Charlotte began to explain, until her brother Lord John Dunford cleared his throat, stopping her in mid-sentence.

Charlotte sighed loudly. What could she say? She could hardly divulge that by tacit understanding between her parents, her father took his long-time mistress to the country estate every year once the Season was over, while Charlotte and her mother stayed in London. It was common enough knowledge that her father had a mistress, but no one knew just how much time the duke spent with her.

How could she tell Archie why she couldn't leave London if John didn't want them to know?

"You are right, Lord Archibald, how remiss of me to forget how shallow I am."

Sarah gasped, but Charlotte ignored her, focusing instead on Archie. Although most of the time she hated him, part of her loved their exchanges. No one saw her as more than a wealthy duke's daughter, to be caught for marriage and used for her hostess skills, and to provide an heir. Those wanting to marry her included false flattery and flummery in their way of talking to her; Archie never did any of that. Even if he only noticed her flaws, she liked how he treated her as a person, not as the daughter of a wealthy duke.

"Not shallow, Lady Charlotte, only too self-centred and focused on London," Archie replied, injecting humour into his voice.

Charlotte ignored the tone. She got some perverse pleasure out of sparring with Archie in public, and she wouldn't be backing down.

"Oh, *self-centred*? Really? Even better." She snorted inelegantly.

Archie just smiled at her, in a most agreeable manner. That annoyed her even more than a cutting reply would have done.

Charlotte had just opened her mouth for a blistering rejoinder when Sarah intervened.

"How is your brother, Archie?" Sarah asked, linking her arm with Charlotte's.

Charlotte looked down at Sarah's hand and realised she was being cautioned to be quiet. She noticed Archie's face pale slightly and wondered why that was.

"He is not so well, I thank you for asking, Duchess," he murmured. Sarah leaned forward and tapped him with her fan again.

He smiled reluctantly and fixed his mistake. "Sarah," he said.

Charlotte inhaled sharply at the exchange. How did Sarah know how to tease him, to make him smile?

All Charlotte knew how to do was to annoy him. Maybe she should try hitting him with her fan? Her fingers tightened reflexively on her new silk adornment. She knew she could never flirt so blatantly with Archie.

"What ails your brother?" Charlotte asked, wondering what everyone else knew that she didn't.

Archie's posture went rigid as he met her gaze. He had the most beautiful brown eyes.

"Arthur left for a grand European trip almost ten years ago. After a few years of travel, he came down with a lung illness that has kept him overseas. The doctors believe that the damp British climate will only worsen his condition."

Archie spoke so stiffly that it seemed a rehearsed speech.

How many times had he repeated that exact phrase? Was his brother so unwell? Still?

"So, is that where you disappear to every year once the Season is over?" Charlotte asked, not thinking about how much that would reveal about her.

Archie gave her a quizzical look, but instead of answering, just inclined his head.

Charlotte flushed and tried her best to conceal her discomfiture.

"I must go. Mother said she wanted to leave early tonight." Charlotte excused herself and moved away from the group, promising Sarah she would visit soon.

When she looked back, she noticed that only one person was looking after her. Archie.

~

Read on here:
https://books2read.com/u/br16Lw

www.ingramcontent.com/pod-product-compliance
Lightning Source LLC
Chambersburg PA
CBHW071818190726
48292CB00005B/1511